The STU Reader

For Michelle + Brian

The STU Reader

Poetry, Prose, and Fiction by St. Thomas University Writers

Edited by
DOUGLAS VIPOND
and RUSSELL A. HUNT

love,
Doug
Kelvin Reunion weekend May 2012

Spelling, punctuation, and formatting have been altered in some places
to achieve consistency across selections.

Edited by Paula Sarson.
Cover design by Jaye Haworth.
Cover images: stock.chng.com
Interior page design by Jaye Haworth and Julie Scriver.
Printed in Canada.
10 9 8 7 6 5 4 3 2 1

Library and Archives Canada Cataloguing in Publication

The STU reader / editors: Douglas Vipond and Russell A. Hunt.

ISBN 978-0-86492-613-5

1. Canadian literature (English) — 21st century. 2. College
verse, Canadian (English) — New Brunswick — Fredericton.
3. College prose, Canadian (English) — New Brunswick — Fredericton.
4. St. Thomas University (Fredericton, N.B.).
I. Vipond, Douglas II. Hunt, Russell A., 1940-

PS8235.C6S78 2010 C810'.80921378715515 C2009-906114-7

Goose Lane Editions acknowledges the financial support of the Canada Council for the Arts, the Government of Canada through the Book Publishing Industry Development Program (BPIDP), and the New Brunswick Department of Wellness, Culture, and Sport for its publishing activities.

Goose Lane Editions
Suite 330, 500 Beaverbrook Court
Fredericton, New Brunswick
CANADA E3B 5X4
www.gooselane.com

For Anne
—*Russ*

For Jane
—*Doug*

Contents

Introduction

Almost from the moment St. Thomas University announced plans for centenary celebrations, an anthology of writing was high on the priority list. What better way to acknowledge STU as a place where reading and writing are not just valued, but are the core of what we do? What better way to celebrate the writers—from "occasionals" to award-winning professionals—who have attended or taught at STU?

And so, this book. We sent out a call for submissions in spring 2008 and before long we had a boxful of poems, short stories, journalistic pieces, memoirs, and essays, all previously published and all written by people who have attended or taught at St. Thomas. The problem of course was to decide which ones to include.

We decided on the William Shawn approach. When Shawn was editor of the *New Yorker*, he said that what he was looking for was simply "good writing." Similarly, we tried to select good writing that would appeal to a broad range of readers. Therefore we excluded specialized academic and professional writing (even though that's what faculty members here and elsewhere mainly do). We looked instead for interesting and entertaining work by people who have one thing in common: St. Thomas University.

This anthology could easily have been several times longer. Except for poetry, we decided to use only one contribution per writer, though that often meant having to choose one of many worthwhile pieces. As the notes on contributors show, STU writers are often prolific. Then, too, there are undoubtedly fine writers whom we have, regretfully, overlooked altogether.

We wanted *good* writing. We weren't, for instance, looking for pieces specifically about St. Thomas University, although, as it happens, several do indeed have STU connections: Stewart Donovan's elegy for English professor Fenton Burke, portraits of well-known alumni (Jenny Dunville on "Mama" Alice Mokoena, Mark Giberson on Harry Forestell), and Carla Gunn's account of lessons learned in the lockout/strike of 2008.

Neither were we looking specifically for writing about New Brunswick. Again, though, it is perhaps not surprising that some of the selections could be classified "New Brunswickiana." In these pages we celebrate the St. John River with David Folster, visit a Maugerville auction with Philip Lee, and, with Tony Tremblay, reflect on the signal importance of the mill in towns like Dalhousie. Bill Spray gives us a tour of historic Fredericton, while Carole Spray shows us why the folk stories and legends of the province are vitally important and worth sharing. Two of the pieces—a poem by Andrew Titus and a magical story by Lorna Drew—have a lot to do with trees. We really *are* in New Brunswick!

A large number of selections focus on individual people—family members, friends, and others. Fathers figure prominently in Dan Gleason's "The Man from Murphysboro," Al Pittman's "Boxing the Compass," and Wayne Curtis's "Fall of '58," while Sheree Fitch writes of her sister in "Cop" and Victoria Kretzschmar Eastman presents a child's-eye view of a slightly scary aunt. In "The Prince of Fortara and The Flat Earth," Ray Fraser recalls his friend Alden Nowlan, and Chris Weagle reflects on a Korean friendship in his poem "Kim Hyo-Sung." Jackie LeBlanc paints a word portrait of Elvis impersonator Mike Bravener, and, as already mentioned, there are close-ups of "Fin" Burke and other St. Thomas characters.

STU writers do not shy away from major world events and social issues. Helen Branswell reflects on the natural history of the SARS epidemic of 2003. Peter Smith muses on the slow expiration of prejudice toward gays and lesbians, a matter also touched upon by Stewart Donovan in "The Gift of Life at the Wandlyn." Darker moments of family conflict, even violence, underlie Nela Rio's short story "El Jardín de las Glicinas" ("The Wisteria Garden") and Sheree Fitch's poem "Edna Remembers Exactly How It Goes."

St. Thomas University is English-speaking, but other languages are spoken, written, and read here, as well. We therefore thought it appropriate to include French and Spanish creative writing in translation. The source and translated works are presented side by side so readers who are able can appreciate the artistry of both writers and translators. We welcome to these pages four individuals who have no direct connection with the University, but who were involved in these dual-language works: Elizabeth Gamble Miller (who translated Nela Rio's story from Spanish to English), Paul Chanel Malenfant and Herménégilde Chiasson (whose poems in French were translated by Marylea MacDonald and Jo-Anne Elder, respectively), and Fred Cogswell (who collaborated with Jo-Anne). Note that the Spanish language is also celebrated in Norma Jean Profitt's meditation on her transformative experiences in Costa Rica, "Of Particle and Wave."

Good writing can be funny. We are delighted to reprint for the first time Leo Ferrari's wonderfully arch defence of Planoterrestrialism, the key tenet of the Flat Earth Society (and see, incidentally, Ray Fraser's piece for an eyewitness account of how the Society began). And don't miss Ian Brodie's brilliant parody of a Socratic dialogue, Sheldon Currie's riveting "Lauchie and Liza and Rory," Gary Langguth's postcard stories, or Kathy Mac's sonnets about dogs with personalities to burn.

In short, the governing principle of this collection is variety. Rather than organizing the pieces into thematic sections, we've foregrounded that variety by interspersing essays, stories, memoirs, poems, and journalism. But whether you read the book from beginning to end or browse through it, prepare to be alternately entertained, amused, enlightened, provoked, charmed, and moved.

The STU Reader. As the very title suggests, this anthology is not just about the fifty or so writers who have contributed to the book.

Equally, it is about readers and reading. We're reminded that the act of writing by itself is incomplete: writing requires reading and response to complete the transaction.

So, dip in, enjoy. The STU writers have done their part; now it's over to you. After all, you are not just holding it—you *are* The STU Reader.

RUSSELL A. HUNT
DOUGLAS VIPOND

St. Thomas University
Fredericton, New Brunswick
June 2009

The STU Reader

Edited by DOUGLAS VIPOND and RUSSELL A. HUNT

Sold!

PHILIP LEE
Saltscapes, 2007

Early one evening in late summer, just as the mosquitoes begin rising from marshes along the banks of the St. John River, we park our cars and pickups six rows deep in the dirt lot, two deep on the lawn, and shoulder to shoulder all the way out to the highway. We have come from points up and down the valley to a warehouse in the community of Maugerville, on the outskirts of Fredericton, to take part in what has become a weekly ritual in these parts: Mark Sloat's Thursday night public auction.

There's a buzz of excitement in the air—we're all here on a treasure hunt of sorts. Most of us don't know exactly what we're looking for, but we have faith the auction will help us find it.

Inside, the set-up is always the same: stacking chairs in rows in the centre; hot dogs, hamburgers, doughnuts, tea and coffee in the canteen at the back. The regulars sit in the front; women are knitting on their laps, men snacking from their lunch boxes. At the counter by the door, Cheryl Edney, Sloat's long-time colleague, hands out the catalogue sheet and yellow numbered bidding cards.

Serious bidders find seats in the back rows, stand on the sides, or roam the room restlessly, inspecting various lots, taking care not to draw attention to the items they want to buy. In fact, they often will inspect with greatest care the items they are least interested in buying. I am not a serious bidder, although I would like to be, so I join the restless set on an inspection tour, trying not to look too interested in the L.L. Bean fly rod I find leaning against the back wall.

My problem as a bidder has been hesitation in the heat of the moment. Hesitate even for half a second and rival bidders stay in too long, thinking your resolve is weak. On this night, however, I have a wily veteran beside me. For Patricia Williams, the auction is her "Saturday night out." She is here almost every week, moving through the crowd in a floppy, broad-brimmed hat. She has a table at the Sunday flea market in Fredericton and is a bargain hunter, hoping to find someone else's treasure.

"If it's sold here, it's not forgotten," she says. "Here, somebody else gets to take it home and enjoy it."

Williams knows that hesitation is my Achilles heel. Acting as my coach, she tells me to get a number in my head, bid hard till I reach it and then get out. If it's meant to be, it's meant to be.

Shortly before six p.m., Mark Sloat enters the room and begins working the crowd, chatting with the regulars, welcoming newcomers. He is forty-four years old, has short brown hair, and is dressed casually in khakis and a golf shirt. His ancient form of commerce is a remarkably efficient way of buying and selling—he completes about one hundred sales an hour. There are no returns. It's up to the buyers to inspect items before bidding, although Sloat is careful to point out the cabinet door that sticks, the old kitchen table "with some age on it" that needs refinishing.

Along with its efficiency, the auction is as honest as the day is long. The people who assemble on any given evening determine the market value of each item. Over time we find great buys, and sometimes pay too much for things we really want. Our house is filled with items of both kinds: we have a Leonardo daVinci reproduction in an old ornate frame that I bought for $175; we also have a $15 "like new" recliner in the living room.

There are many fine auctioneers in eastern Canada and New England, but few stage a weekly general sale. Sloat auctions cars, farm equipment, antiques, art, china, and collectibles, and that's often just in the first hour. The event draws together people from all walks of life: antique dealers and farmers, art collectors and flea market vendors, book collectors and tradesmen. For a time, we are all dancing together to the auctioneer's song.

On this evening, there are 419 lots, arranged in order around the front and sides of the room. On one side I find fuel cans and light bulbs, fishing flies and a motorcycle pocket watch, Royal Doulton figurines and baseball cards, a Maytag washer and Husqvarna chainsaw.

Along the front toward the auctioneer's podium there's a blueberry rake, a coil of rope and a church pew, a broad axe and trumpet, a Hardy Perfect fly reel, and a history of the Miramichi Fish and Game Club.

Down the other side I find a cheque writer and a washstand, a bear trap and two Boy Scout hats, an old highback rocker and a new La-Z-Boy recliner, a Cornwall ornate pump organ and a Crown Staffordshire pedestal cake plate—and an L.L. Bean fly rod and case.

If you can't find something you could use in this room, you need to check your pulse.

At six p.m., Sloat turns on his microphone, welcomes the crowd, and lays out the rules: it's an unreserved auction and therefore everything will be sold; all items must be removed from the building by noon the following day. He will perform for the next four hours without a break, and he will hold this crowd's attention with his voice that he trained when he quit his managerial day job at Zellers to attend the Southwestern Ontario School of Auctioneering.

After graduation, he worked full-time for Cameron Industrial, Inc., a company specializing in industrial auctions. In 1993, Cameron started holding weekly auctions as a way to generate cash flow between industrial sales, and four years later Sloat bought the company. Now, the weekly auctions are his main business. In recent months he has landed some of the most valuable estate sales in New Brunswick, selling fine original art and antiques for tens of thousands of dollars, taking international bids on the phone.

Sloat launches into his cadence, "Okay, here we go, item number one, a box of ceramic figures, lots of good pieces in there, what do you say, $20 for the little box of ceramic, 20, 20, 20, $10 for the box..."

"You want to get a sort of a beat going," Sloat says. "You're singing but you're not singing. This helps create some excitement in the room."

Trevor Smith is standing to the right of the podium. He operates a small antique shop and the auction is his main source of inventory. He says the sound of Sloat's voice is the draw. I look down the front row. People are tapping their toes to the rhythm. "What do you say, $10, we've got 10, now 15, we've got 15 in three places, you're all out, 20..."

Smith would rather come here than go to the movies. "Every week there's something exciting," he says. Last week he purchased a "box of miscellaneous," a favourite buy for bargain hunters. He bought the box for a china teacup that turned out to be cracked. But when he dug to the bottom he found a new portable vacuum cleaner and a salad chopper. "It happens regularly," Smith says. "It's the story of auctions."

Sloat is hitting his stride. The items are arranged so that the first are just warm-up sales to get the audience used to the sound of his voice. The most valuable pieces are sold in the middle of the evening, the bargains at the end. It's all about energy and pace, and the standard auctioneer jokes.

On a cracked porcelain mixing bowl: "A nice item for a high shelf."

On an end table with a cracked leg: "Good from afar, but far from good."

On the commode: "You'll need that. It's a long drive home."

Sloat works the room with his voice, eyes—and intuition. Serious bidders communicate with him using almost imperceptible nods and shakes of the head. "Once you've been doing it long enough, you can be looking in the totally opposite direction. You can feel it in the air and you turn around and make eye contact with someone and know they want to bid," he says.

Gary Price and Roy Bowmaster are standing on opposite sides of the room, picking up items without breaking a sweat. Price, fifty-eight, a retired CP rail conductor, and Bowmaster, seventy-three, a retired cattle rancher and heavy equipment operator, are best friends.

Early that morning they loaded Price's 1985 Chevrolet pickup with its black-and-white camper and drove the back roads from Perth-Andover to Fredericton, a three-and-a-half-hour drive south through the river valley if you're in a hurry, which they weren't.

"There's some beautiful communities along the back roads," Price says. "Today was perfect." A light breeze was blowing when they parked underneath a stand of sugar maples. They broke out the camp stove and fried steak, mushrooms, potatoes; they boiled tea and had doughnuts for dessert. They arrived in Maugerville about four thirty, with lots of time to inspect the items and boil another pot of tea on the tailgate.

"You never know what you're going to see," Bowmaster says. "He's a real good auctioneer. If it calls for a joke, he puts it in there."

"He's one of the best," says Price. "I've been going to auctions all my life on both sides of the border. I've never seen an auctioneer like Mark."

In the past they've purchased an old lariat that was once used for roping cattle ($35), a set of cast iron cornbread pans ($15), some hand-painted dishes ($10) and two old wood planes that were once used to make moulding ($20).

Outside the big bay door, Tim MacAfee is sitting with friends on handmade wooden lawn furniture (it will sell later in the evening), eating hot dogs and drinking coffee. He collects pottery, old stoneware, and earthenware. "We're all custodians of things," he says. "We'll pass them on to the next generation. We are doing a service to society." The group on the bench laughs.

Late in the evening, I move on the L.L. Bean fly rod I've been watching. I put the number $50 in my head. Patricia Williams tells me to get into the bidding at about half that number. Start too low and I'll bring too much company along for the ride. Bidding is competitive and some people buy things at auctions they never intended to buy (we've all done this), getting in at the bargain level and then forgetting to drop out.

I'm in at $25. I make good eye contact with Sloat. No hesitation this time. And then about a minute later I'm the owner of the rod, for $55, plus tax and a 10 per cent buyer's fee.

Half an hour later, the last item sells and the curtain falls. In the parking lot, Price and Bowmaster are loading the old truck for the trip back up the river valley. MacAfee is walking out to his car with an armload of bread pans, an electric griddle, and a stoneware crock. Another man is carrying an old cream can and a bag of golf clubs.

Every week little pieces of Atlantic Canadian history are dispersed back into the community. These are all local estates that are being auctioned off and, rather than the collections being trucked off to another part of the country, they remain in the community. Each piece has a story, and there's a sense that the auction of an estate is the beginning of a new chapter rather than an ending.

I toss my new fly rod into the back seat, ease the car off the grass and turn onto the highway. The city lights reflect off the river as the auction dancers drift off into the darkness of the night.

Cop

SHEREE FITCH

In This House Are Many Women and Other Poems, 2004

Undercover prostitute,
she walked Toronto streets
where she learned the difference
between psychopathic and pathetic
that vanilla
mixed with brown paper
stirred with rain
was the stench of loneliness
that eyes filled with a film of glue
could spill down upon spit-polished boot tips
that tears could come in the midst of city scum.

She found three children
crouched behind a couch
in fear of drunken fists
in the midst of shards of blinking lights
where the tree had crashed down upon
an almost normal family's Christmas Eve.

Another time, she was the first
arriving at a crime
where a ten-year-old

abducted on her way to school
lay bleeding in a ditch
later, at the hospital
tried to give the mother
some reason why
and this was back home
in the Maritimes.

She does all the usual stuff as well
gives out parking tickets, speeding warnings
locks up the city drunks especially in the winter.

Days off, she works with power saw
clears the brush from land she bought
fishes for trout
rides her horse
as she dreams about the home
she'll build
so for a while forgets
the world she walks in.

When she was my kid sister
she was told a girl could not be a cop
but my sister never let
a little thing
like "no such thing"
make her stop.

Today she visits
gun on hip
I meet her
pen in hand.

Sisters:
we will the wor(l)d away
in ways that we know how
hold on to hope
as best we can.

Lauchie and Liza and Rory

SHELDON CURRIE
The Story So Far..., 1997

I knew he'd take her in. I couldn't predict it, mind you, a minute before it happened, but when it did I said as a person often does: I knew it. Once it got to the point, he had to.

She wasn't even good looking. I can say that because she looked an awful lot like me. Red hair. Not the kind that glistens and goes good with green sweaters, but the other kind that looks like violin strings made of carrots. It had a part in the middle looked like an axe-cut, and it was pulled back hard and flat and tied at the back in a little ball you'd swear was nailed to the back of her neck. The same way I did it myself. She didn't exactly have buck teeth, but when her lips were closed her mouth was a little mound like she was keeping an orange peeling over her teeth. When she opened her mouth to talk you could see her teeth were round, and big, and almost the same colour as her hair.

My brothers were identical twins, but as people they were day and night. Liza married Lauchie, the one everybody said was the good one. I could of told her, but I didn't. Even Mother, a smart woman, thought Rory would be a gangster even after he went to work in the pit like everybody else. "He won't last," she said. "He'll get fired, if he don't get killed first, doing something foolish." One Friday in the winter he left with a quart of rum and a dozen beer and a smile and never showed up 'til a week from Monday, out of a taxi, a cast on one leg from toe to hip, a smile on his face, two crutches, and two poles, and one ski.

"You fool," I said when I got him in the house and sat him down on the sofa. "You can't ski."

"Whyn't you tell me that 'fore I left?" he said, and, of course, the big smile.

"The beginning of the end," my mother said, with her eyebrows.

Lauchie went steady with Liza six months. Then he took her home to meet me and Mother and Rory. Soon as she laid eyes on Rory she knew right then she made a mistake. How she knew I don't know. There wasn't a hair of difference between them. Rory knew it too. He shook hands with her. He never shook another person's hand in his life. He put out his big paw and she put her little red one in it, and he put his other hand on her shoulder; you could see her sink under it a fraction. You could almost see her eyes lock into his. "You'll like living here, Liza," he said. "It's a lot of fun if you look at it the right way."

"We'll not be living here," Lauchie said.

"Oh," said Rory. "I thought you were, next door, when the MacDonnells move out."

"Well, we are," Lauchie said, "but there is not here. This is a duplex. Two different houses; one building."

"Some say it's a duplex," Rory said. "I say it's a company house."

"Well, what's the difference?"

"Difference is simple," Rory said. "In a duplex you can't hear people drink water on the other side."

Lauchie wouldn't marry her 'til the MacDonnells moved out, so we had six months to watch her trying to make up her mind. Of course, she couldn't be sure Rory loved her. He might of been laughing at her. With him you couldn't tell for sure. I could, but I'd been watching him for years. Every time she came to the house he shook her hand, and he curled his middle finger so it stuck in her palm, but he did it so it looked like he was making fun of Lauchie, how formal he was when he introduced them. "Rory," he had said, "may I present to you my fiancée, Liza." And Rory shook her hand, like he did every time after, even after the marriage, and said, like an Englishman in the movies, "Awfully good of you to come," and everybody about doubled over laughing, except, of course, Lauchie and, of course, our mother; she stood there and waited for things to get back to "normal."

So Liza and Lauchie got married; Mother died—"mission accomplished, I suppose," Rory said. And they lived across the wall from us and honest to God we never heard a peep out of them 'til their kid was born. Then we heard the kid. They called him Rory. He cried for two years.

When he stopped, Liza started. Both our stairs went up the wall that separated us and I first heard her through that wall, sitting on her stairs, sobbing. After that I took to going over every day to console her, but she never admitted to anything, though she knew I knew. She caught on pretty quick how much alike we were. She talked about it one night we were playing cards, which we did every Friday. "If me and her," she said, meaning me, "if we got our X-rays mixed up, they wouldn't be able to tell which one had T.B." We all looked at her but Lauchie; he looked at his cards.

"What's it mean, anyway, T.B.?" he said.

"Tough biscuit," Rory said.

"You wouldn't need an X-ray to figure that out," I said, thinking to make a joke, but when I looked to Liza for her little smile, she was crying, and I knew there was no secret between us.

When little Rory was five and about to go to school they left him with us on the miner's vacation and went to Halifax to visit Liza's sister and get Lauchie's lungs looked at. "The little bugger needs a little fun before he goes to school," Rory said, and gave him every minute of his time, took him everywhere, showed him everything he could think of, even took him down the pit and showed him where him and his father worked.

When Lauchie and Liza came back, the boy wouldn't go back with them. They had to drag him back. Then he started school and every day he came home he came to the wrong gate and landed in our place. Lauchie would have to come over and drag him back.

"I thought I told you to come straight home."

"I forgot," he'd say.

He kept it up 'til we locked him out. We had to, to keep Lauchie from getting desperate. But he'd start again every time he went through a new phase of growing, until he got to be nine, and after that he wouldn't do his homework except at our place. He hated school, but he was first in his class because he did so much homework. Of course, Rory helped him; he couldn't resist; and when he got to grade nine and Rory couldn't help him anymore he started to teach big Rory. He taught him Algebra, French, Latin, Geometry, Chemistry, English, and God knows what all. He used to bring home the exams and Rory would do them and make high marks. "If I'd a known I was that smart I'd a stayed in school," he'd say. "Probably coulda been a teacher."

Of course he'd show off in the wash house and turned it into a big joke.

"What did you learn today, Rory?" somebody'd say.

"Today I learned that the sailor loves the girl," he'd say.

"And what have you got for homework?"

"For homework we have the girl loves the sailor, but I know it already, puellam nauta amat."

"What would that be in Gaelic?"

"In Gaelic, I couldn't say. I'm a Latin scholar. You'd have to ask me grandmother."

But he wouldn't carry it too far. He knew Lauchie felt bad and Rory wasn't a mean man, no matter how much he liked to make fun.

Once young Rory got to high school his home was nothing to him but bed and board. He had his tea first thing in the morning and last thing at night with us. He went into his side of the house for meals and bed. Nothing to do about it; he was too big then to make him. Liza sat on the stairs and sobbed. Rory felt bad but nothin' he could do, and he couldn't help it that he enjoyed the boy so much. I just watched. I knew something had to happen.

When it happened, it happened very quietly. Of course, that was Liza's way; but I was surprised; I expected a big fight; after all, seventeen years is a long time.

When young Rory graduated he got a big Knights of Columbus

Scholarship and off he went to college. Liza picked the worst day she could find. It was coming down in buckets. She took her big suitcase and a kitchen chair and sat in the road between the two gates in her Burberry and big-rimmed felt hat. It was the first time she ever looked beautiful. It was a Sunday. Both men were home. She went out after Mass and Rory and Lauchie, each in his own side of the house, opened the front doors and watched through their screen doors as she sat there in the mud. In those days there was no pavement, or even a ditch; the road came right up to the picket fence and she sat at the edge of it between the two gates. Talk about a sight. I can still see Rory standing there, peering through the screen, cup and saucer in his hand, sipping tea. And Lauchie on the other side, the same. I knew he would be. I just went over to check.

"What do you think, Lauchie?" I asked him.

"I think it has to be up to him."

And so it was. About six o'clock, Rory said to me, "You better go and tell her to come in. She'll stay there all night."

So in she came. Put on dry clothes and sat and had tea. She cried. They were tears of joy. She was ashamed of them, but couldn't help it. "I realize," she said, "that I'm probably not making anybody happy but myself. I can't help it."

After a few days when we all got the feeling it was settled for good, I moved over with Lauchie.

"Are you mad, Lauchie?" I asked him.

"Nobody to be mad at," he said. "I'd like to be mad. But, you know, it's not Rory's fault. He didn't encourage her; you know that. Just the opposite. Same for Liza. She tried for seventeen years. It's not my fault. It's nobody's fault. Unless it's all our faults. It should of been fixed up seventeen years ago when it started wrong. We all knew."

I certainly didn't know he knew.

"Well," I said, "young Rory will be surprised when he comes home for Christmas."

"I wonder," Lauchie said. "He's supposed to be smart, too. I don't imagine college'll take it out of him that quick."

Kim Hyo-Sung

CHRIS WEAGLE
Malahat Review, 2002

For forty minutes each early morning, we drove
through what seemed like Dr. Eckleberg's wasteland,
to the generator repair plant where I taught
intermediate English lessons to a class
half-filled with beginners. Our time was of silence
and empty stretches; the simpler questions were all

recycled, and our grasp of each other's language
was too basic, and the day was far too early,
to talk about much else than music and food.
Each winter's day we drove past empty icy plains
that melted into fields filled with workers' backs bent
in the sowing and then reaping of radishes.
The silence between us I grew to understand

as less a want of common ground perhaps,
and more the lack of interest in small talk.
But in two seasons' worth of words we shared,
I watched seedlings grow, and valued their beauty
in early drives through farmland in a country
where buildings are stacked up sideways like cards in decks.

That spring, cabbages and radishes began to grow
on the fertile ground of tilled and tended landfill,
in topsoil as secretive as your thoughts could be,
hidden under your placid face, and as we grew
to shift less in our seats, I realized that those
earliest questions we'd long since discarded
had become root beds of calm and quiet friendship.

Boxing the Compass

AL PITTMAN

An Island in the Sky: Selected Poetry of Al Pittman, 2003

The sky is slate grey
threatening rain.
Wind south-southeast.
Maybe more south-by-south-southeast.

The difference could be crucial.

When I was a child
my father took me
around the compass
hundreds and hundreds
of times.

"Boxing the compass" he called it.

Evenings at the kitchen table
he'd draw the compass
on a piece of paper
and have me memorize by name
the thirty-two points from
north to north-north-west-by-north.

We didn't live on the sea then.
And his own ocean-going days
were all long gone.
He drove a car to work.
I walked to school.
The mud-rutted road defined his direction.
The brambled short-cut path defined mine.

But evenings after supper
as though my life depended on it
he'd sit me down beside him
where with a plate from the cupboard
and my school ruler he'd draw
the compass for the thousandth time.

Dusk after dusk
he'd test my memory
until I walked around
inside the house
on the road
in the fields
up the brook
with the compass
spinning this way and that
inside my head.

And sitting in school
through multiplication and long division
through the Ten Commandments and the Beatitudes
through the Crusades and the War of 1812
through the conjugation of latin verbs
through the poems of Bliss Carman and Pauline
Johnson
I wound around the compass like a clock
gone giddy with turning.

In the middle of his middle age
I bought my father a boat and a compass.
We moored her in the shelter of a small cove
where she could come to no harm
while at rest between her little league voyages
up and down the unhazardous shore.
But even when she was tied up
going nowhere bouncing gently
up and down and around her mooring
I'd see from back aft
my father in the wheelhouse
standing spread-legged.
The wheel in his calloused grip.
His eyes glued to the compass.
And I wondered then
if he was out somewhere
in a bank of fog on the Grand Banks
rolling in a south-east wind
remembering.

Once upon a time
in a fog bank on the Grand Banks
his younger brother went overboard.
And though they searched all night
they couldn't find him.
When the fog lifted at daybreak
they looked again.
But no luck.

My father and my uncle
their brother gone
forever to "the grey seas under"
took their course
and headed south-south-west-by-west
to Boston.

His boat is long gone
to the sand and the seaside grass.
But I still have the compass
he used to navigate his last voyage
to nowhere.
It sits on a stand
in a corner of my living room.
I check it often
each and almost every day.

Remembering SARS

HELEN BRANSWELL
The Canadian Press, March 6, 2008

He's given his SARS talk so often, and in so many parts of the globe, that Dr. Donald Low can still rhyme off, to the day and the date, exactly what happened when during the four-month international disease crisis caused by severe acute respiratory syndrome.

The Ontario government declared an emergency on March 26, he recalls without checking notes. A mothballed TB unit at West Park Hospital was converted into a makeshift treatment unit on March 21 for the first wave of Toronto health-care workers who contracted SARS. "Every time I give the talk—and I've given the talk hundreds of times—it's unbelievable the impact it has on the audience," Low says in an interview marking the fifth anniversary of the outbreak that claimed forty-four lives in Canada. "And it doesn't matter whether it's epidemiologists, infection control, public health people, or lay people—the story is so compelling."

If many remain fascinated by SARS five years after it burst onto the pages of medical history, only a few people in southern China were paying attention when the story actually began. It was November 2002 when people started getting sick with a severe respiratory illness in the province of Guangdong. It would take awhile for the nascent disease to ping on the global health radar.

Surging vinegar sales in China grabbed the attention of the folks who regularly scour the globe for what might be budding disease outbreaks, like those who work for the Canadian-led Global Public

Health Intelligence Network. “We were getting lots of rumours, like a lot of sales of vinegar,” explains Dick Thompson, who was the spokesperson for the World Health Organization’s communicable diseases section at the time. “Vinegar in southern China is used as a disinfectant. And so if there’s a run on vinegar, there’d be a suspicion that there was some kind of infectious disease or a widespread belief that there is an infectious disease outbreak. So at these meetings we’d been hearing this kind of drip, drip, drip come in about that.”

The early signs had experts thinking pandemic influenza, which to flu scientists is what “the big one” is to seismologists. The last pandemic was in 1968. Were these the first rumblings of the next big one? In mid-February of 2003, Mother Nature threw the anxious watchers a red herring. Several members of a family from Hong Kong contracted H5N1 avian influenza while in China’s Fujian Province—the first time in six years human cases of the feared strain of flu had been recorded. That turned out to be an unrelated coincidence.

In the years since the SARS outbreak, scientists have concluded a coronavirus that normally infects bats found its way into civet cats—a raccoon-like animal eaten with gusto in some parts of China. These unfortunate intermediate hosts transferred the virus to humans, it is believed. Somewhere in this chain of events a mutation took root in the virus’s genetic coding, ramping up the intensity of disease it caused. In humans, SARS was nasty; nearly one in ten of the nearly eighty-one hundred probable SARS cases died, which in disease terms is very high.

A problem percolating in China spilled out across the world in the third week of February, when international travellers were infected at the Metropole Hotel in Kowloon, across the harbour from Hong Kong. A gravely ill Chinese doctor checked into Room 911 of the hotel. When he later went to hospital—where he died—the doctor infected health-care workers and triggered the largest SARS outbreak outside of mainland China. But he also infected travellers who took the disease to Hanoi, Singapore, Taiwan, Vancouver, and Toronto.

In Vancouver, doctors quickly realized what they were dealing with and instigated precautions that kept the disease from spreading.

But all the other cities suffered large outbreaks after the disease infiltrated hospitals. The Toronto woman who brought the disease to Canada's largest city died at home and infected multiple family members. All the infections in the region traced back to this poor woman's chance encounter with a new virus in a Kowloon hotel.

By late February, Dr. Carlo Urbani, a WHO infectious diseases expert based in Asia, alerted the Geneva-based agency that the disease had spread beyond China. Urbani himself became infected with the virus and died in late March. On March 12, the WHO sent out an unprecedented health alert warning of a new "atypical pneumonia." By the fourteenth, a Friday, Canada and Singapore were also reporting cases, Dr. David Heymann, then WHO's executive director of communicable diseases, recalls. "We were very afraid that it was a [flu] pandemic developing," says Heymann, who is now an assistant director-general for health security and the environment.

The next day Heymann, Thompson, and Denis Aitkin, a senior official in the office of then-director general Gro Harlem Brundtland, huddled to name the new disease. "How many times do you get the chance to name a disease?" Thompson recalls, his voice still tinged with wonder. For Heymann, the experience wasn't a first. He had been on the team that battled the first reported outbreak of a new hemorrhagic fever in Zaire, now the Democratic Republic of Congo, in 1976. The scientist who led that team, Karl Johnston, had been insistent the name should not forever stigmatize a town, so the dreadful disease was named after the nearby Ebola River instead. "We wanted it to be similar to AIDS—to have a name...and an acronym but also a description of what it was. So respiratory, severe...those things we finally put together into SARS," Heymann explains.

While the trio in Geneva was naming the disease, scientists at the National Microbiology Laboratory in Winnipeg began tests on specimens from Toronto. Polymerase chain reaction—PCR—tests can only find known disease agents; the test searches for genetic material that matches samples it has been programmed to look for. "So we put it through our chlamydia test and our flu test and all the other viruses that we thought it could be....And they all came up negative. Then we kind of more or less knew we were into unknown territory," says scientific director Dr. Frank Plummer, whose lab now boasts new technology that can search for the DNA of unknown disease agents. "For the National Microbiology Lab, it was really a defining moment," Plummer says of the SARS outbreak. "It really thrust us onto the world stage."

In Toronto, Low and the army of other people who never became household names initially didn't realize how far SARS had spread. Staff of the first hospital—Scarborough Grace—had been infected. So had patients who were located near the first case to come into hospital, along with their family members. People who didn't know they had been infected with the new disease turned up at other hospitals, where staff had been told to be on the lookout for people who had recently been to China. And patients who would too late be identified as SARS cases were transferred from Scarborough Grace to hospitals around the greater Toronto area. Like sparks from a fire, they soon set off their own blazes.

Nurse Susan Sorrenti was on duty when one such patient was transferred to Mount Sinai Hospital. She caught SARS. Sorrenti, who still nurses, agitated at the time for higher levels of precaution—a position that would later be taken up by Justice Archie Campbell, who conducted the exhaustive investigation into SARS ordered by the Ontario government. Campbell, who died last April, just three months after issuing his massive final report, stressed that the precautionary principle must be used in future outbreaks—when in doubt, opt for higher levels of protection, he said.

"I guess it taught us all a good lesson about what we think we know. From the top guys on down," Sorrenti says. "Big, big lesson. Big price."

The virus behind the disease was identified at the United States Centers for Disease Control in Atlanta. And shortly thereafter Vancouver's Michael Smith Genome Sciences Centre became the first lab to map the genetic code of the SARS coronavirus.

The public health researchers rushing to reveal the virus's mysteries to help the containment effort found themselves working against the clock, with an anxious world peering over their shoulders.

Plummer describes it as "doing science under intense public scrutiny. You're responding to press conferences that are being held in Hong Kong twelve hours earlier. So it's very different. You're kind of getting further and further out on a limb, actually."

At the time, public health measures long abandoned, quarantine and isolation, were dusted off and pressed into service. These old tools earned new respect because of the disease's particular quirks. It had a long incubation period and people weren't infectious until after they got sick, so there was merit in telling those exposed to stay home until it was clear they were not infected. Less admired—by affected cities, anyway—were advisories issued by the World Health Organization, in which the agency urged people to avoid cities where SARS appeared to be careering out of control. Heymann still justifies the measure, insisting the WHO felt it was necessary to curb travel. "Our biggest fear was that it would get into a country where it was missed in surveillance," he explains. "And the other fear was that it would become endemic in some animal population and constantly reinfect humans."

In reality the warnings were only formalizing what was already happening. People were already shunning locations where SARS was spreading. In Toronto, movie shoots were relocating, large conventions were cancelling, and hotel vacancy rates were soaring. Still, the travel advisory issued April 23 infuriated Canadian officials. Toronto's then mayor Mel Lastman, seemingly unaware of the World Health Organization or at least its acronym, angrily demanded "Who is WHO?" in an interview on CNN.

Ironically, by the time the travel advisory was issued, Toronto was past the worst of the outbreak—or so it appeared at the time. Authorities in the city were actually breathing collective sighs of relief. That's because the previous weekend had been Easter, a pivotal point in the battle. Several members of a Filipino religious group had fallen ill. Authorities were fearful the sacred rites of Easter would further spread the disease and churches were asked to suspend practices that might further transmission, like the passing of the communion cup.

"We got through the weekend basically holding our breath, doing all we could to obtain as much information as possible and to react to it," recalls federal health minister Tony Clement, who was Ontario's health minister at the time. "And the number of cases started to decline. So that was when we knew that we could beat this infection and it wasn't going to go through the whole community."

Canada celebrated too soon, however. Believing the outbreak was over, authorities told health-care workers they could remove their hot masks and respirators. The smouldering embers of the outbreak again burst into flame, causing a second wave of infections. A further 90 people were infected and 12 died during the second phase of Toronto's SARS outbreak. In the two waves combined, Canada recorded 375 probable and suspect cases of SARS. Two nurses and a doctor were among the 44 people who succumbed to the disease.

New Waterford Boy

in memoriam Fenton Burke, 1942-2001

STEWART DONOVAN

The Molly Poems and Highland Elegies, 2005

Was it 1949 or '50 when one of your schoolmates
Missed the intended target
And sent that snowball
Through the neighbour's window?
The shattered glass gleaming like Waterford
Crystal as it fell in icicles around the baby basket.
Your companions fled,
But you in your innocence and faith stayed,
If not guilty you never ran, there's nothing to fear.
It wasn't the blow or the shattered teeth you recalled,
But the weight of that half-mad and simple man
Pressing down on your eight-year-old chest.
    And, later, the figure of your father, Big Frank Burke,
    Pacing the kitchen linoleum like some caged cougar
In sight of her young.
Your mother and his fellow miners filling the air
With quiet desperation, hoping
Frank won't kill the man.

Ah, Fin, what were the odds of getting out?
And how many times were you warned
That being blessed with brains

Was no ticket to the girl
And the job and the home back home.

Some miner's son swallowing Latin phrases
Could easily end up in the seminary or become,
Like your cousin, a Scarborough missionary casually
Martyred in Santo Domingo.
But for you it would be summers in Shilo, polishing
Leather, cleaning small arms, reading tactics, taking
Orders and smoking endless cigarettes under those
Ocean prairie skies.

Your folks understood
The army as a job Maritimers so often took,
But when the COTC ended how did you
Explain the possibility of a life in literature?
Classroom, class and counter-class.
Was it 1991
When we visited the small park and monument
Above the pithead of Number 12 Colliery—all
Those forgotten lives.
You had nothing to say
Other than it wasn't the Waterford you'd known.
And how had you changed?

What would a flashback of thirty years of teaching tell
Anyone about the boy-man
Who moved from early Elvis to Merle Haggard and lived
As gospel Franz Kafka's belief that
The book was the axe that broke the frozen sea
Inside us all?

Parsley and Pink Petunias

GARY J. LANGGUTH
Gaspereau Review, 1997

Lil Chaisson bought old Dave Johnson's purple Pontiac for two hundred bucks and of course the thing died as soon as she pulled into her yard. Poor Lil is soft-hearted, so she never said anything about it. What she did do is get into the gin with the daughter and the two of them stumbled down here at two in the morning, borrowed two shovels and proceeded to fill the trunk with dirt. Lil is ashamed about the whole thing and has planted parsley and pink petunias in the trunk and whenever Dave asks about the Pontiac, she always says it looks great.

Isabella, Double-You Be

■ KATHY MAC
Event, 2008

Haw-eyed, dudley-nosed, floppy-flewed, cheer-leader ingenue,
your shoulders and tail zig while hips zag, then change
zag zig zag, again again again; you careen along
quoting Lady Di's chin-down gaze, peering up through

curly strawblonde-and-cream (liver-and-white)
at the sound of your many monikers: Dizzy Miss Izzy
Isalator, Bellisisima, W.B. (for Wiggly-Bum, or Wanna-Be).
Fur, matt-invitingly ample, shampoo-model bright,

in your plushy "Bella Buzz," this summer's hot 'do.
Despite how you moan, I won't paint your nails;
you'll just chip them, bouncing through bushes, over rails,
after the other "bunnies." Like a drogue anchor,

you're towed home, where you collapse, boneless,
and sleep like you're suctioned to the ground.

"I Am a St. John River Person"

DAVID FOLSTER

New Brunswick Reader, November 25, 1995

> Of the many rivers of northeastern America, it would be difficult to find one which, in the diversity of its natural features, the facilities afforded for sportsmen, and the interesting history of its colonization, is more worthy of mention than the St. John; and yet this river, viewed in its entirety, has never formed the subject of any published work.
>
> — J.W. Bailey, 1894

Some things have changed since Joseph Whitman Bailey wrote those lines 101 years ago. For one, there have since been a few "published works" about the St. John, notably by W.O. Raymond, Esther Clark Wright, and Bailey himself. But his central thesis of a century ago remains intact: it is still one of North America's grandest unknown rivers.

One night about twenty-five years ago I was having dinner at the Beaverbrook Hotel in Fredericton when a man walked in who I thought I recognized from television as a recent candidate for mayor of New York. Fretting through my meal, I finally got up the nerve to go over to his table and ask. Sure enough, William F. Buckley, Jr., looked up at me.

I was, of course, anxious to know what he was doing in Fredericton. But all Buckley and his entourage of eight or nine wanted to talk about was the St. John River. I gathered they had just seen it for the first time. They raved about its beauty. They wanted to know about the islands below Fredericton and whether the trees that line their perimeters so symmetrically had been planted or had grown naturally. What the Buckley group simply couldn't understand was why they hadn't heard about this splendid river long before this.

Joe Bailey's answer to that question, in 1894, was that the river's lack of renown was due to its international dichotomy—"the fact that the area drained by it lies partly in the United States and partly in Canada." The result, he said, was a bad case of mutual envy:

> The patriotic Canadian does not care to eulogize the vast wilderness of northern Maine, which, if the assertions of provincial geographers are true, was unjustly carved out of New Brunswick by the much-abused Ashburton Treaty. The American, on the other hand, is not very eager to expatiate upon the natural resources of a country that he might prefer to possess as a fractional part of his own.

Perhaps there are other reasons. I have friends who declare it is better that we keep our greatest natural asset to ourselves, lest we are overrun by defilers and despoilers. My own suspicion is that the St. John isn't better known because we at home have been slow to grasp what a truly significant geographical entity our river is—and, moreover, that it also has a metaphorical quality that is right for the times.

Consider first its physical dimensions. Its watershed is huge, embracing one state and two provinces. It occupies fifty-five thousand square kilometres, an area larger than Switzerland and about the size of Nova Scotia. Fourteen major tributaries—among them the Allagash, Madawaska, Aroostook, Tobique, and Kennebecasis—and hundreds of small streams are part of the system. It also has some very large lakes, including Maine's Square Lake and Long Lake, Quebec's Lac Témiscouata, and New Brunswick's Grand Lake.

Writing in the early 1900s, Reverend Raymond, an Anglican cleric, historian, and author of *The River St. John*, said the river was 750 kilometres long from the deep Maine woods to the Bay of Fundy.

"No river on the Atlantic Seaboard, south of the St. Lawrence, has such magnificent reaches and lake-like expansions as the St. John or can compare with it in the extent of navigable water," he declared.

Today, Canada's National Atlas Information Service puts the length at 673 kilometres. That makes it the second longest eastern seaboard river between the St. Lawrence and the Gulf of Mexico. It is exceeded only by the Susquehanna, a river which rises in New York State and follows a serpentine course 715 kilometres to Chesapeake Bay in Maryland. The St. John remains longer than the Hudson, Potomac, Connecticut, Merrimack, Delaware, and the Suwannee, too.

A big difference, though, is that the St. John has never had a Mark Twain, Stephen Foster, or Henry David Thoreau. Well, that's not quite true. Thoreau did once venture into the Allagash country, and there was also the young Englishman—a Thoreau wannabe, perhaps —who went into the Tobique territory in the fall of 1851. His is an amazing tale that, like many involving the St. John system, is practically unknown.

Hiring Indian guides to take him far up the river, the Englishman's solitary mission was like Thoreau's at Walden Pond: he thought any philosopher worth his salt ought to spend some quality time in the forest depths, "where the very wilderness around him would teach him truths he knew not of, would murmur mighty secrets in his ear."

The Britisher got truth and secrets in spades. Sitting in the gloom of his ten-by-ten forest cabin, he wrote in his journal: "It is no life of idleness. This chopping of fuel has become to me like the money-gathering of a miser; even as he is tormented by the constant fear of want and starvation in the winter of his fears, so have I ever in mind the dread of winter before me."

His food supply dwindled and he had to shoot a squirrel, "one of my confiding, fearless, humorous little friends." Persistent rain, "clattering on the cedar roof like the scampering of a hundred mice," brought up the river and carried away his canoe; he was left a prisoner of the trees, his "jailers." But even as despondency seeped into his "smoky, lonely, leaky-roofed camp," he ruminated eloquently on the glories of pine and hemlock, and cast his prescient vision ahead to a time when there would be homesteads, gardens, even "the sweet tinkling of a church bell" o'er the Tobique.

Our New Brunswick Thoreau finally did escape on the river ice just before Christmas, leaving us with a journal—and a mystery. Published in London fifteen years later, the journal identified the author only by his initials—J.M.C. So we know neither his name nor, as it happens, his fate. All we have is a publisher's oblique observation that, after surviving his trials on the Tobique, "his few added years of life were doomed to pass in struggles of a different kind." And by the time his book appeared, he was dead.

When a small group of us formed the St. John River Society in 1991, it was precisely so that we might celebrate our history and make stories like J.M.C.'s better known. That's why at 12:15 p.m. on June 24 each year, at the society's instigation, churches all over the valley ring their bells to mark Samuel de Champlain's naming of the river on the Feast Day of St. John the Baptist in 1604.

But the pealing bells also resonate with a larger symbolic purpose. To appreciate it fully, you must let your mind wander...think about churches...the Cathedral on the Green in Fredericton; a country church at McDonald Corner near the Washademoak; Catholic churches across the river from each other in Fort Kent, Maine, and Clair, New Brunswick; another on the shores of Quebec's Témiscouata; and, yes, even a gleaming little Protestant church on the Tobique (whose bell is one rescued a few years ago from a mothballed steam engine)...imagine these churches, and others, ringing their bells at the same time, all being part of something that binds us together. That *something* is the St. John River. It is the uncommon river we have in common.

No doubt Joseph Whitman Bailey would be pleased with this new cross-border symbolism of shared purpose and interest. Nor are church belfries the only place it can be found. A recent river art competition drew entries from more than fifty painters on both sides of the border. And an annual River Rhythms concert on the grounds of Old Government House in Fredericton brings together performers from up and down the valley in a celebration of music, song, and dance devoted to water and rivers.

The first to appreciate the full glory of the St. John were, of course, the Aboriginal people. They knew the river well, describing its course with remarkable accuracy to the earliest European incursionists. They also gave it a wonderfully descriptive name, *Wolastoq*, which in English means "good and bountiful," a phrase still apt even in the late twentieth century.

People of many other ethnic origins have followed the Aboriginal people up the river in the last four hundred years: French, English, and Irish; the Swedes who founded New Sweden, Maine; the Danes of New Denmark; the Scotch Colonists; Dutch; German; and so on. This gives us a sense of the river not only as geography but as metaphor, too—a link among people of different cultures, origins, and jurisdictions. Surely this is a healthy idea in a world growing more fractionary; and thus does the united pealing of the bells become even more poignant on June 24.

For my part, I take a romantic view of the river, and I find the romance is enhanced by considering the river system in its entirety. I like the notion that some of the water running past my home at Island View originated "way up there" above Lac Témiscouata or as a tiny spring bubbling to the surface on the side of Mount Carleton. In spring, I find inspiration in the unfolding drama of flood season, knowing that what is happening in the deep, dark woods of Maine will, in a few days, determine the river's look, size, and performance at Fredericton.

In Maine, the St. John is a wilderness river, running wild and free through great tracts of spruce and fir. By the time it reaches Fredericton it has been tamed (or so we like to think), harnessed by three major dams, and is smoothing out for its gentle estuarial ride to the sea. But here's an interesting thing: the river rises in northern Maine at roughly the same latitude (forty-six degrees north) it returns to 570 kilometres downstream at Fredericton, having flowed in a steady northeasterly direction for about its first 200 kilometres before turning southward at Edmundston.

This means that, early in its journey to the sea, the St. John introduces its watchers to a river-long propensity toward spectacle. It comes in the spring, too, the unofficial beginning of the river-watching season for aficionados. Because of its more southerly location, the melting upstream ice sometimes lets go before the more northerly downstream ice. When that happens, the results can be spectacular.

More than half a century ago, a pretty young schoolteacher from Fort Kent, Helen Hamlin, got a job instructing the children of loggers at an isolated Maine lumber camp on the river's upper reaches. Out of this three-year wilderness sojourn came a book, a regional classic called *Nine Mile Bridge*, and a vivid description of a typical spring breakup that began as a faint upstream roar as she and her husband stood transfixed:

> A ten-foot wall of tumbling, crackling, fast-moving ice rolled around the upper bend of the river, sweeping everything before it, gathering momentum and throwing two-ton ice floes on the high banks.... It was breathtaking, and I hung tightly to the bridge railing, unable to tear my eyes away. The ten-foot wall grew to twelve feet, then to fifteen, and thirty feet from the bridge it angrily greeted us with an ear-splitting screech. Curly touched my arm and I turned away. The spell was broken and we started to run.

Hamlin describes stepping off the bridge just as the ice hit, then watching from a knoll as the huge cakes shook the ground and tore the wooden bridgeheads like kindling, a moment of inherent drama we can all appreciate. Ice runs on the St. John are spectacular, as are the following freshets, unless you happen to be in the way, as thousands have been (sometimes repeatedly) over the past two hundred years.

At Grand Falls, the spectacle is the ice tumbling over the falls and the tonnes of water roaring through the gorge below. Somewhere in my accumulations is an old 8 mm film, taken in the folly and recklessness of youth at the bottom of the steps leading into the gorge, the spring freshet at its height and the foaming torrent barely a couple of metres away from the camera lens. The last time I looked at the film, it still scared the daylights out of me.

What is remarkable, though, is that precious little of this drama has been recorded along the St. John, especially in written form. Helen Hamlin's book is part of a very small body of St. John River literature. Or so it seems. Perhaps a bibliographer should be set to work on the task of determining what really is out there. There may be some surprises. John Steinbeck, for example, ventured into the territory of the St. John for *Travels with Charley*, and Grey Owl, the Englishman turned Indian turned conservation writer, spent time near Lac Témiscouata.

Is it also possible that, like the Hudson River, the St. John has engendered a distinctive style of painting, but without anybody noticing? Such "schools" are born in various ways. One I became acquainted with a few years ago at Skagen, at the northern tip of Denmark, was said to be the result of the peculiar quality of the available light at this spot where the Baltic meets the Atlantic.

Is there also something artistically distinctive along the St. John? The green lushness of the valley in summer, perhaps, or the crystalline combination of white and blue in winter? Maybe the answer will emerge, in time, from the St. John River Society's annual river art competition.

In music, a body of work does exist, but again one must seek and find and listen. Its entries include everything from the recent Phil Nimmons composition "Riverscape" to "Tater Raisin' Man" by the late Dick Curless of Fort Fairfield, Maine, an uptempo hymn to the trials of potato farming (and a better song than "Bud the Spud"). It could also include a piece by Robert Nobles of Hatfield Point. He went to the western states where he became Bob Nolan of the Sons of the Pioneers and wrote the western classic "Cool Water." Who's to say that its invocation of "cool, clear, water" wasn't inspired by memories of the great river he grew up beside?

As for contemporary paeans to the St. John, none can compare to "Back to the River St. John," written and sung by Janet Kidd of Saint John. Having seen the river and absorbed some of its stories from her in-laws, about people who move away and always long to come back, Ms. Kidd told herself: "I bet I could write about that gorgeous river."And so she did—in about sixty inspired minutes.

With her Irish sensibility and poetic skill (she was born in Dublin), she composed a lilting song about love and nostalgia for the river. It may yet become the watershed anthem.

What all of this art, music, literature, history, beauty, and sociology add up to is a St. John River mystique. We have it, but true to our Canadian upbringing, we never speak of it. By contrast, the Americans, including those who live along the St. John in Aroostook County—"The County," as they say—imbue practically every square foot of their turf with mystique. Here's a test: think of any American state; I'll bet some image of that state pops into the mind almost immediately. I once asked a professor friend of mine if he could think of any exceptions and he said, "Well, Arkansas." And then he added, "New Brunswick is like Arkansas, with fish." But that was before Bill Clinton.

The Americans have turned mystique into an economic force. We have not—which might reflect a becoming modesty but, more likely, reflects a failure to grasp and celebrate our own history and culture. Instead, we appropriate ersatz versions of American culture. Examples abound: merchants donning cowboy suits for sales promotions, poolside Hawaiian luaus and "Malibu" parties, and, saddest of all, a newspaper photograph just the other day of a Maliseet, a descendant of people who did some of the most exquisite beadwork on the North American continent, wearing a feathered headdress, just like in the (American) movies.

The strange thing is that we seem to have lost our way and fallen into cultural denial only in the last 100 years or so. Before that, our image (of ourselves and to others) was sharp and clear. We were the place of "iron men and wooden ships" and, later, of "the big woods" and the best fishing and "big game" hunting—meaning moose and caribou—in all of eastern America. Royalty, Gilded Age entrepreneurs, sports figures, and even the occasional actor and actress came here to disport themselves. Then we lost it, and by the 1980s our confusion about who we are was so great that the provincial government actually commissioned an ad agency—in New York, of all places—to create an image for us. Naturally, it failed.

A true image, whether for a person or for a geographic area, comes not from the drawing board but from the soul. The collective soul of the St. John River is our shared history and culture, and it is rich. From where I am writing this, I can see just a small stretch of the St. John, and yet my vista is filled with cultural and historical icons. Directly out in front is Sugar Island, so named because it was once covered with sugar maples, and was the scene, in 1786, of an incident in which a patronage claimant to the island was met by a band of twenty-one armed men and "turned out in a violent manner," as historian Stewart MacNutt wrote.

Butternuts and wild St. John valley grapes grow there. Fiddleheads, the quintessential New Brunswick symbol, grow on the next island, Savage. It's also where Maliseet once convened annually to deliberate and to have canoe and foot races. Just opposite, on the river's other bank, is Currie Mountain, an old volcano, now a UNB protectorate and the place where some of the province's oldest white pines stand.

So it goes up and down the valley and into the tributaries. The point is this: we are a people blessed with a great river and many holy places along it. It pervades our lives, whether we realize it or not.

I once had a tour of Dublin with a guide who kept proclaiming, "I am a Dublin man." It had a nice ring to it, a proud sentiment born of deep affection for his city and its history. So should we say, "I am a St. John River person." *J'ai le fleuve Saint-Jean dans le sang.* We are all river people. The river is us. We are the river.

Et la saison avance

■ HERMÉNÉGILDE CHIASSON

Climats, 1996

Et la saison avance
Les radios jouent plus fort
Les arbres sont plus longs qu'avant
Le plafond est plus blanc
Et la saison avance
Le jour est plus court
Les arbres sont plus blancs
Le plafond est plus beau
La rue est plus large qu'avant
Et tu me cries
Et je cours inlassablement vers toi
C'est ridicule
Je sais
Mais la saison avance
Le jour est plus court
C'est ridicule
Je sais

And the Season Advances

Translation by JO-ANNE ELDER
and FRED COGSWELL
Climates, 1999

And the season advances
The radios are louder
The trees are taller than they were
The sky is whiter
And the season advances
The day gets shorter
The trees are whiter
The sky is more beautiful
The street is wider than it was
And you cry out to me
And I run towards you untiringly
It is ridiculous
I know
But the season advances
The day gets shorter
It is ridiculous
I know

Giving Up by the Goleta Slough

TONY STEELE
Impossible Landscapes, 2005

I trail behind the others down the grassy path
from the cliffs to the beach. The world
like a woman's body, a woman's body like
the imitation of an earth. I pause and look
back into the folds of the ravines
at the curled, hairy, dry brush
around the sides of the canyon.
Where the path opens to the rock-piled beach,
I see the only red flower on the path.
And near it a yellow mushroom.

I don't remember when I first started abdicating.
But now I am no longer a writer and interested only
in making sure each word is different, the paper
begins to look holy again. It looks like the yellow
sheets of rough draft my aunt composed
in my sister's bedroom when I was twelve:
the product of a magic brain, no longer entirely my own.

I can tell when the moment of sunset has come
when the silver tops of the olive trees turn dark.

The Dialogue of Socrates with Hero

IAN BRODIE

The Nashwaak Review, 1995

The scene takes place outside of Socrates's barber. It provides a prologue to the shave and haircut dramatized in the earlier work, The Cereal Bowl. *There is no doubt that Hero was a real person, like the other named characters in Plato's dialogues, but it is unnecessary to believe that he was really this stingy.*

The dialogue is in two parts: the first introduces a definition for happiness which Socrates analyzes and then discards; the second proposes the concept of the external forms (or Forms) which is given in more detail (or Detail) in further works, most notably The Phaedo. *The brevity of the dialogue is unusual, but it is believed that Plato was requested to "keep it at around a thousand words."*

SOCRATES: Why, hello, Hero! What brings you to this bench at this time of day? The sun is at its peak, and yet you are not performing some task befitting your station.

HERO: I'm having lunch. It's a nice day, so I'm eating outside.

SOCRATES: Ah, I see. *(He sits in contemplation for a few moments.)* Um... are you going to finish that hoagie?[1]

HERO: Certainly, without question.

SOCRATES: All of it?

1. A colloquial term for a sandwich served on an elongated bun, consisting of lettuce, cold cuts, tomatoes, cheeses, and various sauces and garnishes. It is similar to a submarine, yet it is not heated (a submarine may be served hot or cold).

HERO: Emphatically so.

SOCRATES: Ah. *(A pause.)* It is a big hoagie though, isn't it?

HERO: Yes it is, and I am going to finish it. I've had a really bad morning and I have classes all afternoon. The only bright spot of my day will be this hoagie. I've looked forward to it all morning long.

SOCRATES: So, what you're saying is that this hoagie will bring you happiness?[2]

HERO: Yes. It will.

SOCRATES: So you define happiness as the completion of a big hoagie?

HERO: I am not practiced in the ways of logic, my dear Socrates,[3] but I will say that, for me, at this point in time, happiness is the eating of a big hoagie.

SOCRATES: But is this true in all cases? Take for example a well-fed man. He often has hoagies, but he may still be unhappy. Is this not so?

HERO: Sure, whatever.

SOCRATES: For him, happiness may take the form of some antacid and a nap. A man, just coming out of a year-long coma, on the other hand, would find a nap most unappealing, and would just want to catch up on how the Blue Jays are doing. Or am I wrong?

HERO: I'm not sure.

SOCRATES: Remember what the poet[4] said:

I get no kick from champagne.
Mere alcohol doesn't thrill me at all;
So tell me why should it be true
That I get a kick out of you?

2. The introduction of the dialectic.
3. Meant to be sarcastic. From the dialogue, we learn that Hero is a lethargic, skeptical acquaintance of Socrates, prone to fits of near hysteria. Not much is known of Hero, except that he is the basis for a small character in Aristophanes's *The Toast-Rack*, in which he is described as "puckishly handsome / cute 'n' cuddly." This is mentioned in the Chorus, so, of course, no one takes it seriously.
4. Cole Porter, although often erroneously attributed to Jimmy Van Heusen.

Doesn't that show another form of happiness, without even mentioning hoagies?

HERO: Okay, so I was wrong. Sue me.

SOCRATES: I do not want to offend you. I am trying to gain knowledge. Many years ago, Chaerephon,[5] a friend of mine from boyhood, went to the Oracle at Delphi,[6] and asked whether there was anyone wiser than myself. She said, in that enigmatic way of hers, "No."

HERO: Yeah, I've heard that.

SOCRATES: Ever since, guided by her words and by this little voice in my head, I have vowed to search for any wiser than myself. I do this by asking questions.

HERO: How nice for you. Tell me, does this little voice in your head tell you to go around annoying people trying to eat their lunches?

SOCRATES: *(Ignoring him.)* You see, there's this cave.[7]

HERO: *(To himself.)* Oh, no.

SOCRATES: And in this cave, there are varieties of cold cuts, mustards, lettuce, cheeses, tomatoes, and breads. But the cave is dark, and the prisoners (for that is who inhabit this cave) are chained, and can only look at what lies before them. Besides, they have no knives or cutting boards. One day, a prisoner is released, and he makes his way out of the cave. At first, he is blinded by the brightness of the outside world, but he soon comes to realize that he isn't actually in the outside world, only in the kitchen of a deli. He is amazed by what the short-order cooks can do, especially with pickles, but in no time at all he can make a Zero Mostel, the house specialty, in less than three minutes, complete with fries and cole slaw. He

---

5. One of the few democrats in Socrates's circle, also appearing in *The Clouds* and its lesser-known sequel, *The Inclement Weather Condition*.
6. Well, duh.
7. The earliest known reference to the cave mentioned in *The Republic* (514A-521B). An earlier dialogue mentions the "Myth of the Cavity" (Dr. Shapiro, DDS, 14C).

returns to the cave but he finds it so dark that he can't see where he is going. The other prisoners laugh at his disorientation, and when he tries to explain the intricacies of a Reuben[8] they slather him with mayonnaise and poke him with his paper hat.[9]

HERO: *(After an uncomfortably long pause.)* So what's your point?

SOCRATES: Can you really sit there and say that happiness is a hoagie?

HERO: *(Infuriated.)* No, I can't, at least not now. Thanks to this conversation I'm late for class, without having finished lunch. You've proven that I don't know what happiness is, but I have a pretty firm grasp on the notion of tardiness. Have the damn hoagie! *(He exits.)*

SOCRATES: Yummy! I love hoagies! Heh, heh, heh, I'm getting good at this.

HERO: *(Returning.)* Damn, damn, damn!

SOCRATES: What's the matter? You don't want your hoagie back, do you? I've licked it all over,[10] but if you...

HERO: No, keep it. But I can't find my keys.

SOCRATES: What do you mean?

HERO: I don't know where my keys are.

SOCRATES: You don't know, or you can't recollect?

HERO: Okay, I can't recollect. Are you sitting on them?

SOCRATES: *(Again in his own little world.)* Do you know what they look like?

HERO: What?

SOCRATES: What do keys look like?

HERO: You know...keys! Uh, metal, roughed-edged things on a metal loop.

---

8. Pastrami, Swiss cheese (or mozzarella), and sauerkraut on rye.
9. The prisoner, of course, refers to Socrates. The paper hat is Crito, and I shall refrain from explaining whom the mayonnaise refers to, as it's all so tawdry. Suffice it to say, "corrupting the youth" was not entirely unjustified.
10. A bad habit of Socrates, attributed to Xanthippe's use of custard on everything she prepared. He ate little else, which may explain his crankiness.

SOCRATES: But is this always the case? To a pianist, a key is an ebony- or ivory-covered piece of wood and a succession of eight notes. To a mariner, it's an artificial landing place, and it's spelled differently.[11] To a locksmith, it's food on the table, clothes and shoes for the children...

HERO: Uh-huh, but mine are for my apartment and mailbox.

SOCRATES: Exactly. So there must be some sort of perfect "keyness" which at one time we have all encountered, against which we measure all things "keylike."[12] Whenever we see something in this world with an element of "keyness," we immediately say to ourselves, "Ah, I know what that is. That's a key." This can be proven by giving a set of keys to a simple slave boy, and then locking him in a room. Not only will he be able to escape from the room, he can hum "Duelling Banjos" in G sharp with no musical training. This all leads to the inevitable conclusion that when we are born, our souls somehow forget all that we have learned in previous lives, such as "beauty," "piety," "important phone numbers," and, of course, "keyness." Our lives must be spent, therefore, trying to recollect that which we have forgotten.

HERO: That is truly fascinating, but I still can't recollect where my keys are. Have you seen them?

SOCRATES: They're in my pocket.[13]

HERO: What!?!?

SOCRATES: *(Pulling them from his pocket.)* I had them all the time. All you had to do was ask.

---

11. Quay. I bet you feel really dumb.
12. A huge leap in logic, but then again, this was one of Plato's earliest works, and it shows.
13. Another bad habit. Although he claimed to be completely law-abiding, records show he was often caught doing sneaky things. Indeed, scholars believe that his persecution was instigated by Meletus after Socrates taped a large "Kick Me" sign to Meletus's wife's back. She, coincidentally, bore a striking resemblance to a hoagie.

HERO: I did!

SOCRATES: No, you asked if I was sitting on them. You never once asked, "Socrates, are my keys in your pocket?" or "Hey, Socrates, did you take my keys?" You see, that's why I ask a lot of questions. Not only do I seek wisdom, but I never lose track of things.[14]

HERO: May I have them back, please?

SOCRATES: Certainly. Now I must be off. Goodbye, Hero. I hope we may speak again sometime. You may teach me something yet. *(He exits.)*

HERO: *(To himself.)* Good riddance. I'm already late for... what? What the...? *(Calling after Socrates.)* Hey! Socrates! Where the hell's my wallet?!? *(He exits.)*

14. He may have a good point, but remember, he never had anything to lose.

Fishbones

ROGER MOORE
Ariel, 1991

Each day, all thumbs, I braid my daughter's hair:
I can manage two bunches, one on each side,
but it's much more difficult to part it neatly into three
and to work for that one thick plait she loves down her back.
As for fishbones and French braiding...
She begs me to try; and I promise that when my thumbs
have turned to fingers, I'll give it a go.

Out in the garden, onions push their stubborn way
through dancing daffodils. It's easy to make mistakes:
they were all just bulbs when my mother planted them.
Forget-me-nots twine intricate designs—a fantasy
of reds, greens, and blues,—between runner beans.
I pull them apart with clumsy fingers, yet they knot
like tangles, fresh each day, in my youngster's hair.

Last winter, a heavy snowfall toppled the garden wall.
Bricks and mortar litter the grass in untidy piles.
I hold my child by an arm and a leg and swing her round,
faster and faster till, dizzy, she can hardly stand.

Now she staggers like my father who stumps on two front
sticks and jabs at the wall he wants me to rebuild.
Spittle dribbles from stroke-slackened jaw.
He claws, with twisted hand, at words,
like fishbones, caught in his throat.

The Mill Was All in Northern New Brunswick

TONY TREMBLAY

Saint John Telegraph-Journal, January 26, 2008

There is a formative moment in Alistair MacLeod's "The Boat" when the son of a fishing family makes the acquaintance of a boat that is the real and symbolic and tenuous centre of his life. It was that way too in Dalhousie, except it was a pulp and paper mill, an eyesore of red bricks and active stacks stretching along the entire length of the front street, that at some point became the centre of our lives, whether our fathers worked there or not.

On January 31, 2008, Abitibi-Bowater shut it down for good, ending a seventy-seven-year history that survived the Great Depression, global wars, countless recessions and buyouts. Ending, as well, a way of life for almost ten thousand New Brunswickers.

The mill was the host organism from which our town fed for three generations. Store owners, teachers, electricians, and firemen owed their living to it every bit as much as papermakers and millwrights. Mill wages, the best in the region, paid groceries and mortgages and tuition, and provided the tax revenue that built roads and rinks, sidewalks and parks.

As the central repository of myth, anecdote, and general concern, the mill was never farther than one degree of separation from everyone in town. If your father didn't work there, your neighbour or uncle did. We owed our life's blood to the mill, and cursed every second we spent in it. That was the paradox of our lives: the tenuousness of an existence beholden to something cherished and despised. We were glad to have the damn mill at the top of our bay, even as it destroyed the lives within it. That the mill always drove a hard bargain was one of our early lessons.

The old-timers claim it was different. Pictures from the 1930s and '40s show them standing by the machines they worked in an age before automation, an age when mechanical know-how made paper —when an extra rinse or a slow dry were the personal signatures of career men who made newsprint by guarded recipes. They could have been medieval guildsmen, these old guys who shared their secrets grudgingly with underlings (fifth hand, fourth hand, third hand) who had proven their worth. The machines they tended might be the horses their own fathers depended on in the camps sixty years ago, they look so proud.

To work in the mill carried status, these photos say, to be a papermaker even more. And among papermakers, the boss machine tender, like a walking boss, was revered most of all. And so the mill's hierarchy became the town's, sectioned by where one worked and how high up he was. Just as the white-shirt operations were always on the highest floors, so were the choicest neighbourhoods on the hills overlooking town. None lived above the mill manager's house; to contemplate it was a breach of form, entertained only by those from away.

The journeymen boilermakers and tradesmen who built the mill in the 1920s stayed on to form the first labour force. Many were skilled immigrants who married local girls. In some cases each had to learn the other's language (language was permeable, religion was not). Their children's inheritance was a job in the mill, a guarantee of relief from a lifetime of frozen hands and feudal impoverishment to the woods and waters. Like their fathers, second-generation workers didn't only learn skills but self-reliance—and from that gained the confidence to live full lives with hope and dignity. In our town, one never had to apologize for working in the mill. To work there was to deepen roots and extend family, solidify the tribe. Those who didn't understand called it ingrown, provincial. Their families broke and scattered.

In those early days, the mill had little choice but to be beneficent.

Some New York industrialist's hefty investment demanded it. "Company houses" were built for workers; a seven-mile pipeline was constructed from the Charlo River into town. The Chaleur Inn, the company's hotel, hosted gala dinners and Christmas parties. Its dining room was legendary, its photographer renowned. In an age before television made standards ubiquitous, it was our Waldorf-Astoria.

In later years, a fire hall was built at the end of the front street, below it a sizeable dock for export. Even an electrical grid was devised. If a transformer blew outside your house, you'd call the mill to dispatch a repair crew. In a time before Louis Robichaud's program of Equal Opportunity reform, NB Power served the cities of the south, leaving towns like ours in the protectorate of our primary industry. It was the same with health care. In the days when J.S. Woodsworth and Tommy Douglas were devising the rudiments of Medicare in Canada, whole families visited the mill nurse, who triaged illnesses and dispensed medication. Those who made sport of snickering at millworkers' sticky fingers, joking at what got carried out in steel lunchboxes, misunderstood this culture of reciprocity—of the mill as host organism, giving as it took. To scold a man for a dozen pocketed screws when the mill had taken his health, hearing, and two of his fingers was to miscalculate the imbalance of the exchange.

Someone from away was always remarking on how dirty our little town was, especially in March when five months of accumulated soot formed an ever-blackening crust on receding snow. Again, they saw more than they understood, for soot was the residue of our success; when the mill made paper, so did the town eat. And eat we did on the mill's schedule: "dinner," the day's big meal at noon, when the shift was 4-12. "Supper" at five when the shift was "days" or "douze-à-huit," 12-8, graveyard.

Likewise with the other schedules in our lives. We set our watches by the mill whistle (noon and five o'clock) and gauged the wind by what we smelled (sulphur or groundwood). There were houses we didn't enter when fathers were sleeping off a shift, Labour Day parades we watched in which every float was made with something recycled from the yard. Our rush hour, inasmuch as we had one, was closer to four than five. Every kid who played minor hockey wore an NBIP jersey and walked from dressing rooms to ice on rubber mats that once were conveyor belts near the pile. The mill was ubiquitous in our lives, always in our ears and noses and under our feet.

The recent announcement of closure marks the end of a gradual erosion of this reciprocity, started a generation ago when gentlemen industrialists sold their interests to calculator-toting MBAs who spoke a language of streamlining and globalization. Loyalties and inheritances gave way to a new bottom line of performance measures and market accommodation. To question the logic of these systems was to be thought Neanderthal or difficult. The days of CIP executives R.J. Cullen and John H. Hinman making twice-yearly visits to fish the Matapédia as honourary members of the Matamajaw Salmon Club were long over. New owners trolled mills like Dalhousie's for fat pension plans, unvested until retirement. Easy pickings for those who'd never once been in our town (or our mill). For those only months or a few short years from retirement, it is surely the most humiliating of the mill's hard bargains.

The town as service district will not die because towns rarely do. Rather, they redesign themselves, usually in more modest guises than previously displayed. But the old town that many of us knew as the gentle and benevolent place of our youth will never live again. And that town is worth remembering. The sense of secure confidence in a lifetime job that translates into large groupings of families living by the dictates of a regimented industrial process is gone forever, and with it the special social configurations of a town designed to accept logs for manufacture into paper.

The rhythms of life will switch to daytime living and comraderies will take new form. Men and families will not know each other in quite the same way as when workers shared shacks and cafeterias, the brotherhood of union solidarity or pride in so many days without accident. Language will change, too, not just the hand gestures used to communicate in environments above ninety decibels, but the mix of English and French so long used by men of different backgrounds working side by side on the same floor.

The richness of the mill's largely oral culture will fade into the past. Nicknames and stories will never be as colourful as when relied on as content to fill long nights and mind-numbing routines. The woods/town interface, so integral to mill operations, will also change, leaving townsfolk without an essential part of their heritage. Fewer people will follow moose birds along southeast logging roads in fall, and fewer still will sit in camps and shanties constructed by a know-how hard won in the mill. There will be no more jerry-rigged heating systems and fewer patchwork houses, their additions appearing at regular intervals after promotions and contracts. Facility with the pole and picaroon will fade into the past.

But most of all there will be no more first paycheques portending a lifetime of employment—no more long horizons of rising fortunes. To have expected that to continue, we are now told, was naïve and unrealistic—as if our town's hopes were impinging on someone's prerogative to invest elsewhere, perhaps where workers are less demanding of what owners routinely enjoy.

The final paradox of our lives is that as much as our fathers and uncles cursed the bastard, they can't bear to let it go.

Yellow Bath

PATRICK JAMIESON
The Gray Door, 2004

Josie, do you recall, as I do, 1965
When your cousin Albert studied
Medicine in this Atlantic city?

We stayed one time in this hotel.
The friendly doorman: Was his name
Horatio? We occupied this very room
Or one just like it, with its muted tone.

You said that the angles,
The grays—even the noises in the hall—
Held this muffled quality.

A yellow bathtub in such a
Context seems happily appropriate.

A period piece of a hotel room,
With twin beds and yellow curtains.

Where did you say Albert lives now?
His daughters, the babies: Did you say
The red-haired one is on the stage?

And the yellow-haired younger one
Is in the military, like her Father?

Their uniforms are sharp and gray.

Collecting the Stories

CAROLE SPRAY

Will o' the Wisp: Folk Tales and Legends of New Brunswick, 1979

I must confess that on the day in 1966 when Dr. Louise Manny tried to persuade me to attend the Miramichi Folksong Festival in Newcastle, I made excuses. I'd heard some of the songs on the radio that afternoon and I didn't feel too keen about attending a live performance. The truth is, I was used to the more conventional modern and classical music, and folksongs sounded uninteresting to me. As for folk tales, I thought I could learn everything there was to know by reading English literature. Being a true New Brunswicker, I felt sure that if there was folklore around here, it probably wasn't significant, and if it was significant, then there wouldn't be much of it in New Brunswick anyway. All of which shows that I knew absolutely nothing about folklore and even less about New Brunswick, although I had lived here all my life.

But I never forgot Dr. Manny. She was the founder of the Miramichi Folksong Festival, author of *Ships of Miramichi,* and co-author with James Wilson of the classic *Folksongs of Miramichi.* Her accomplishments and her great personal vitality and integrity inspired both love and respect. After she died, the thought kept nagging at me that if New Brunswick folklore was important to her, then there must be something in it. Many of the songs had been collected, but I remembered her saying, "There are lots of good stories here." I wondered, what kind of stories might they be? And how could I collect them?

Of course, professional folklorists like Marius Barbeau and Helen Creighton had collected material in New Brunswick for years and this is continued today by Edward D. (Sandy) Ives, Neil Rosenberg, Sister Catherine Jolicoeur, and Charlotte Cormier, to name a few. The songs are not neglected; there are *Folksongs of Miramichi,* Creighton's *Folksongs from Southern New Brunswick,* and if you can obtain a copy of Edward D. (Sandy) Ives's book on Joe Scott, the song maker from Lower Woodstock, you'll be very lucky indeed. But there are few books available in English that deal directly with the subject of legends and folk tales with an emphasis on New Brunswick.

What is folklore, anyway? I wasn't sure what I was searching for and when I consulted *The Standard Dictionary of Folklore,* I found twenty-three separate definitions and that confused me even more. Folklorists themselves can't seem to agree on any one in particular, but I think we can say that folklore is almost any tradition or expression that is circulated informally among members of a group. It includes songs, stories, sayings, superstitions, and recitations. Often the author is unknown and usually there is more than one version.

I began to listen and to talk to people about local folklore and I poked through material in libraries and archives for evidence of tales that had been collected in the past. I found Dr. Manny was right. "There are lots of good stories here." To properly research and collect these stories, I knew I would need a tape recorder, a babysitter, and lots of gas. Fortunately, the Canada Council provided me with an Explorations Grant, and I was off and running.

I started with my relatives. I was delighted to hear my father, Edward Jeffrey, telling stories I'd heard as a child, stories I had almost forgotten. He told me about a man who found Acadian gold in the bank of the Memramcook River, about the treasure supposedly buried under the old Fitzsimmons Reservoir in Moncton, and about the ghost who haunted his old home on Lester Avenue. The ghost wore a bowler hat, a high-winged collar, and a coat with split tails. He used to walk out of one of the bedrooms and down the stairs. His footsteps could be heard and whenever he appeared, you could see right through him. It turned out that the main structure of the old house had once been a barn and a man who faced financial ruin hanged himself from the rafters.

I discovered that my father-in-law had heard about the ghost of an old sea captain who died of the fever back in the days when Irish immigrants landed on Sheldrake Island. The wife of a lighthouse keeper used to see the apparition roaming up and down the shore. He told me how the organ in his house began playing at the very moment when a neighbour killed herself. I learned about the headless nun who haunts Morrison Cove Bridge, and I listened to tall tales about how large the mosquitoes were and how thick the fog was around Miramichi Bay.

After I had exhausted my relatives, I started working on friends and acquaintances. I soon learned that it was pointless to ask "Do you know any folklore?" because most people said "No," but if I said "Do you know any stories or superstitions or cures?" then usually I'd get "Yes" for an answer. A lot of people could think of someone else who knew stories too, and soon I had a long list of people to interview. If I didn't know a person, I'd write a letter to them explaining what I was up to, followed by a phone call and then a visit. Sometimes just a visit would do. In the beginning, I thought it would take three or four sessions before anyone could relax enough to face a microphone. But it didn't turn out that way. With few exceptions, people opened up within the first hour and became so engrossed in the stories they were telling or the songs they were singing that all self-consciousness seemed to disappear.

The first real stranger I interviewed was Harding Smith, an eighty-seven-year-old lumberman who lived in Fredericton but had spent much of his life around Parker's Ridge. "Smiddy" was eager to talk about the old days and to tell stories, and like many older people, his memory for the past was as sharp as a whetted knife. He sang more than twenty-eight songs for me, some of them with verses as long as your arm, and he told of his times in the lumber camps as if it had happened the day before. I saw him every week for over six months because his oral history of early days in New Brunswick was almost as fascinating as the man himself. I'll never forget visiting him in hospital a few days before he died. By then we had become firm friends, and as I sat on the edge of his bed he raised himself up on one elbow and began, "Say, did I ever tell you about Geordie Brown and the pancakes?" He went on for almost an hour, laughing, talking, and even singing, as if it were someone else who carried his pain and as if he had an eternity of bright tomorrows to live. "See ya," he said.

I spent a lot of time on Miramichi. The people are friendly and the area is uncommonly rich in folklore. Once I started in an area like that, I found it was hard to stop because one person led to another all up and down the river, and some people became friends I visited more than once. Most of the stories in this area come from the lumber camps, and that's not surprising since a good proportion of the men who lived along the major waterways in this province made their living as lumbermen.

The men would go into the woods in the fall of the year and not come out until spring. Living together in small isolated communities forced people to rely on themselves for nearly everything. The men sometimes conducted their own funerals, buried their companions in makeshift coffins such as a pork barrel or two flour barrels, and marked the place by nailing a shoepack to a tree at the head of the grave. They devised their own remedies, provided their own entertainments, and commemorated events by making up songs and poems and stories. They sang about the deaths of their comrades such as Peter Emberley and Samuel Allen, about the horrors of the Miramichi Fire and about the joys of Duffy's Hotel.

It was a tough life filled with danger and rewarded with very little pay. If a man wasn't killed by a falling log or washed away by floodwaters, he might slip into the river during a stream drive or take a fall while dislodging a tree. I heard about one foreman who carried a rifle with him on his rounds. When he saw one of his men twenty feet up trying to chop free a lodged tree, he said "If you don't come down I'll kill ya, 'cause I don't want no dead men around here!"

Dead Man Camp was the name given to one lumbering operation near Burnt Hill, New Brunswick. According to this story, a teamster arrived in camp late one night with his horses hauling a full load of logs. Because the road to the landing was very steep and treacherous, the boss told him, "You'd better put your team away and wait until morning to unload." But the teamster was stubborn.

"I'll either land this load, or I'll eat my supper in hell," he said, and away he went as if the Devil himself was after him. The horses missed a sharp turn in the road, overshot the landing and crashed into the river, killing all. The place is supposed to be haunted, and it is said that any team of horses will balk and refuse to proceed down that hill.

Like most of us, lumbermen relied on their own feelings about experience to interpret the cause and effect of events. They were naturally superstitious. It was believed you should never hire on a Friday because whoever was hired then wouldn't stay the whole season, and if a man got a chain knotted, it meant he would quit. A camp built of popple wood was bad luck because Christ's cross was made of popple. To sing the song "Peter Emberley" in camp meant that someone would get hurt. If a man slept with his head facing downstream he risked drowning, and if he went to bed with his axe embedded in wood, he would get no sleep. Teamsters relied on this little ditty when they went to buy a horse:

> One white foot, try him;
> Two white feet, buy him;
> Three white feet, deny him;
> Four white feet and one white nose
> Cut off his head and throw him to the crows.

On Saturday night and Sunday, the men had time off and then there'd be singing and dancing, fiddling and diddling, storytelling and games. Sometimes the games were invented by the men themselves or else they were adapted from games they had learned at home. They included Hot-Ass, Jack-in-the-Dark, Rooster, Shoulder-the-Sheep, Selling-the-Salt, and Shuffle-the-Brogue. In the latter game, the men would sit in a circle around the person who was "It." A shoepack would be passed around under the men's knees. When "It" had his back turned, someone would hurl the shoepack at him and he had to guess who had thrown it. If he guessed correctly, that person became "It," but if he made a mistake, the game continued as before.

One of the most interesting games I heard about was Uncle Allan's Rope Trick. Uncle Allan bored holes through a deacon's bench and threaded a rope through it every which way and then tied the rope in a knot. The men were supposed to figure out how to get the rope out of the deacon's bench without untying the knot. They worked at it all fall, winter, and spring without success. Before the camp broke up for the summer, one of the men came to Uncle Allan and said, "What's the secret of getting that rope out without untying the knot?" Uncle Allan's reply was: "The secret is, it can't be done." The important thing was to give the men something to do.

Like most legends and tales, the stories told by the men grew from their own experience or else they evolved from traditional stories, but regardless of the source, the stories would be expanded or changed a little with each telling. Over the years, as the men moved from one camp or one place to another, they took their stories with them. That's why the legend "The Man Who Plucked the Gorbey" can be found throughout New Brunswick and Maine. Stories vaguely similar to some of those told about Will Lolar are also told in Maine about a character called George Knox who was supposedly in league with the Devil.

Other stories such as "Three Gold Hairs from the Giant's Back" were told not because they had anything to do with the lumber woods, but because of their entertainment value. These wonder tales or *Märchen* tell of giants and fairies and other magical beings, and they are quite rare. They come from many cultures and go back many generations, even beyond the Brothers Grimm who first collected these stories from the European oral tradition. "Three Gold Hairs from the Giant's Back" has been collected before from Wilmot MacDonald by both Creighton and Ives. A verbatim transcript and a good discussion of the story appear in *Northeast Folklore,* volume 4.

In the past, self-reliance was a way of life not only in the lumber camps but also in the general community of the Maritimes. When people were sick, they often had no choice but to cure themselves.

Some of the cures were unusual. If you had asthma the thing to do was to bore a hole in a tree at the exact height of your head. Then, cut off a lock of your hair, put it in the hole and plug the hole. By the time you grew past that hole in the tree you'd be cured. However, if you happened to be bald or finished growing, you could eat field mice fried in butter. Smelly socks tied around the neck, goose grease on the chest, and salt fish bound onto the feet would cure a sore throat, cold, and fever. For rheumatism or arthritis, you might put a piece of copper in your pocket or shoe and sleep with potatoes in your bed. The best thing for a sore back was to find someone who was born at Christmas and get them to walk up and down your spine. The following story illustrates just how effective some remedies could be:

> It was wintertime and this fella's wife had the earache awful bad. She was moanin' and groanin' and 'pon my soul it near killed her. So her husband said, "I'm gonna cure your earache." And she said, "How?" "Well," he said, "just you wait." He went out and he got a stick of white maplewood, and he stuck it in the oven with one end of it hanging down. After a while, the log began to thaw and sizzle and the hot sap began trickling out. The husband caught the sap in a teaspoon and went and poured it into her ear. Oh, it near burnt the head offa her. She jumped out of bed hanging on to her ear with the most awfullest yowling you've ever heard. "My, my," he said. "I think the cure is worse than the disease."
>
> —Horace Hunter, Astle

Since doctors were scarce and home remedies often failed, people would call upon healers and charmers to cure certain ailments. Blood charmers were common everywhere, but the secret of the charm itself was not easy to obtain. There are many variations of this procedure, but usually a man could tell one woman and a woman could tell one man, but if the rule wasn't followed, the power to charm blood was lost. The blood charmer would place one hand on the patient's head and the other hand on the wound. The patient had to speak his full name and then the charmer whispered some words from Ezekiel, whereupon the blood clotted and the wound healed.

In 1881, the New Brunswick Medical Act was passed preventing anyone except licensed physicians from practicing medicine, but this did not include "clairvoyant physicians practicing prior to 25th March 1881." The special status of "clairvoyant physician" applied to the Rev. Harry Price, a Presbyterian minister at Boiestown, who was famous for setting bones, and to Father William Morriscy of Bartibogue.

Father Morriscy was born in Halifax in 1841, and after studying medicine for two years, he trained for the priesthood at St. Michael's College, then served in Caraquet and Bathurst under Father Pacquet, a qualified physician. Probably Father Morriscy learned a lot from the older priest, but the young man possessed a rare gift. He had the uncanny ability to diagnose an illness simply by looking at the patient. By the time Father Morriscy became pastor at Bartibogue in 1877, he was widely known and people were travelling from the United States and from as far west as British Columbia to be cured by him. He used balsam and herbs and other natural ingredients in his remedies and they say much of his knowledge came to him from the Mi'kmaq tribe at Burnt Church.

According to legend, this priest's charity was unlimited. Never would he accept pay for his services and when one patient left a gold coin on his table, Father Morriscy hitched up his horse and galloped after him to return the money. Once in the midst of a violent storm, a call came to him from an ailing Protestant who had been abandoned and left to die. The priest knew from the description of the disease that the man couldn't be helped medically, and since he was not of the same faith the man didn't require spiritual assistance, either. Nevertheless, Father Morriscy started out at five o'clock in the morning and after exhausting three horses, he arrived at the man's bedside at ten o'clock that night. The ailing Protestant died, but not uncomforted or alone.

Father Morriscy's work continued even after his death in 1908, for he left his prescriptions to the Sisters of the Hotel Dieu Hospital in Chatham. They possessed neither the way nor the means to place these remedies before the public and so a group of Moncton businessmen formed "The Father Morriscy Medicine Company," which later moved to Montreal. The cures were marketed far and wide and Father Morriscy of Bartibogue became famous all over North America. As a folk hero, he has been remembered in a number of poems, and one of them entitled "A Christmas Greeting 1885" was written by Michael Whelan, the poet of Renous.

Father Ryan of Red Bank died only a few years ago, and he, too, was famous for his cures. One man told me of how he had frozen his hand when he fell through the ice and the doctor informed him that his fingers would have to be cut off. The man refused such drastic measures and went to Father Ryan for advice. The priest instructed him to soak his fingers in alcohol for an hour each day and put them in pickle brine three times a week. Today the man boasts that his hand is in perfect shape because of the priest's advice. Father Ryan's remedy for rashes was to boil straw in a bucket of water and then use the water for washing, but his favourite cure-all was to bathe in a tub filled with pine boughs and eggs, broken shells and all. According to local tradition, a famous country and western singer came to the priest with cancer of the throat. The man spent all of one summer at Red Bank, and Father Ryan is said to have cured him so completely that he is still a top singing star today.

I doubt that Father Ryan ever pretended to be a licensed physician, but people sought comfort from him and believed in him and, like the good Bishop in the tale "The Woman, the Bishop and the Cow," he did what he could. The patient's improved state of mind was perhaps almost as important in bringing about a cure as the remedy itself. Time and faith were as potent then as they are now.

The stories told about Father Delagarde at New Mills and Benjamin River are almost all examples of faith healing. Many speak with great awe and admiration of this strict but beloved priest. He served the people in this area for almost twenty-five years and when his parishioners called on him, he prayed from his book, laid his hands upon them, and gave firm but gentle words of encouragement. His parishioners tell how he cured one woman dying of tuberculosis so that she lived to raise her many children. They say that a baby who was dying of fever recovered after Father Delagarde prayed over him, and an older child recovered from what was thought to be a case of spinal meningitis. His people speak of him as a "holy priest" and he was buried about twenty years ago near the place where he was born, in Saint-Isidore, Gloucester County.

As far as I know, neither Father Ryan nor Father Delagarde were remembered in song or verse as were some local heroes. Many of the poems I collected were written, like the songs, about murder, shipwrecks, and death, or else they were satires on local characters and events. Usually these verses were simply committed to memory, but occasionally broadsheets were printed and sold in the streets. For instance, in Saint John, a British spectator wrote an epic poem entitled "The Race and the Death of John Renforth" which was sold in the streets in 1871. It concerned the famous boat race between "the Tyne Crew" of England and four men of Saint John, who made up "the Paris Crew." John Renforth was the stroke of the British team and he died of a heart attack in a last desperate attempt to overtake the Paris Crew. The Saint John team won and the poet made enough money from his verse to pay his passage home to England.

The famous Bannister Murder which occurred near Moncton in the 1930s inspired a poem called "The Pacific Junction Tragedy." It was written by C.H. Murray and sold in the streets of Moncton for fifteen cents a copy. Part of it went:

> The day of execution came
> It was an awful sight
> To see those poor brothers
> Marching in the morning light
> And one spoke to the hangman
> These words they heard him say
> "The rope is choking me," he said
> "And I would like to pray."

Some verses were, and still are, recited at concerts and community entertainments. Among the most popular at Miramichi are Hedley Parker's "The Days of Duffy Gillis" and "The Man Behind the Boathook," about early lumbering days and the breaking of the South West Boom. Another common favourite is James Hannay's "The Maiden's Sacrifice," and equally interesting as a recitation is "The Ballad of Margery Grey," a sad lament about a woman with a baby who wanders from the family homestead and perishes in the snow. Some of the recitations came from old school texts and were learned in the era when schools put more emphasis on memory. Others came from anonymous or uncertain sources, such as this saga that Carl Webber of Chipman recites about a man who had twenty-eight names.

I was brought to be christened before I could speak
So I cannot account for this terrible freak
My mother and father were excellent folk
So when I was born they were both of one mind
And they said, "Let us give him all the names we can find."
And so they consented as wise as could be
And this is the handle they stuck unto me:
Jonathan, Joseph, Jeremiah,
Timothy, Titus, Obediah,
William, Walker, Henry, Sim,
Reuben, Rufus, Solomon, Jim,
Nathaniel, Daniel, Abraham,
Roderick, Frederick, Peter and Sam,
Hiram, Tyler, Nicholas, Pat,
Christopher, Dib, Jehosophat.
When I went and got married, the case was so bad
The preacher looked at me as if I were mad
Said he, "Young man, it is a great shame
Your parents denied you a sensible name.
Say nothing more, but for reasons of mine,
You will have to be married a bit at a time."
Jonathan, Joseph... (repeat all names)
When I joined the club, the clerk of the town was calling the roll,
And he ended with my name. And there wasn't a soul
To wait for the end. They all got so vexed,
They said they'd go home, and come back for the rest.

Of course, recitations don't have to rhyme. Some were simply pieces of nonsense prose like this one:

> A boy lost about the size of man. He was barefooted with his father's shoes on. He was born before his eldest brother and his mother was absent at the occasion. His hair was cut curly and he was cross-eyed at the back of his neck. He had on a mutton-chop coat with bean soup lining. He had on his back an empty sack containing two railroad tongues and three bung holes. The last place he was seen was on the courthouse roof shovelling wind. Anybody knowing his whereabouts, please notify his Aunt Ruth.
>
> —Carl Webber, Chipman

Another kind of folk poetry is the jump-rope rhyme heard on sidewalks and in schoolyards, and it provides interesting insights into how children view the world. The simplest is a "plain jump-rhyme" in which the child skips to the rhythms of the verse. This one came from Kathy McDonnell of St. Dunstan's School in Fredericton.

> Miss Monroe
> Broke her toe
> Riding on a buffalo
> The buffalo died
> And Miss Munroe cried
> And that's the end of the buffalo ride.

The endurance or "prophetic" rhymes are more complicated, and they can be quite grisly.

> Fudge, Fudge, call the judge
> Jane is gonna have a baby
> Jack is going crazy
> Boy, Girl, Boy, Girl... (skip until miss to tell which gender)
> Wrap it up in tissue paper

Send it down the elevator
One, two, three, four... (skip until miss to tell how many children)

Children are excellent sources of folklore. Maybe that's because they are generally receptive and more open to imaginative pursuits, and both playgrounds and schoolyards provide group situations where traditions can be passed on informally. Elementary school children love to tell shaggy-dog stories that go on and on and carry a strong punchline, as in "The Ghost of the One Black Eye." And then there are the jokes about the "little moron" or the "Newfie" or yet another variation on the "knock, knock" theme which is so common.

Riddles are very popular, especially among preschoolers who tend to ask the same riddle of the same person over and over again. I wonder if this is because young children are especially tickled by this brand of humour or because they take delight in practicing a new skill or because "one-upmanship" over anyone is a new and pleasant experience.

Superstition in children begins very early, as soon as they begin to notice cause and effect. Whenever the car is stopped at a red light, our children love to chant, "Red, red, turn to green." When the inevitable happens and the light changes, they seem enormously pleased with themselves. It's not that they don't understand that stoplights work by electricity, they just prefer to believe in their own power to influence events. Almost every child knows the old saying "Step on a crack, you'll break your mother's back," and I've seen children as young as three and four go out of their way to avoid walking on cracks in the sidewalk. It is a rudimentary game that coincides with the development of conscience.

The concerns of older children are often expressed in certain folk practices. For instance, a young girl might try to find out who her future husband will be by peeling an apple and throwing the peel over her shoulder. If it falls in the shape of a letter, then that letter signifies the first letter in her future husband's name. Teenagers may try to "raise the Devil" in more ways than one. One method is to read the Lord's Prayer backwards. Another is to go down cellar and walk around counter-clockwise with a white candle seven times. Then, if you look in a mirror, you'll see the Devil over your left shoulder. I've heard plenty about this practice, but nothing about the results!

Although most teenagers possess a keen interest in the supernatural, all of the "serious" ghost stories I collected came from older people, the youngest of whom was in his mid-twenties. In a way, ghost stories were one of the most touchy areas of belief because many of the people who told these stories were firmly convinced of their reality, and were most anxious for me to believe so, too. Personally, I find it very easy to suspend disbelief with even the wildest of tales and I found some of these stories sounded very convincing. I've never seen a ghost myself, but I firmly believe these things do occur. The explanation is beyond me.

Despite the sensitivity felt toward ghost stories and certain beliefs, almost everybody I met was willing to take the time to think of stories, songs, superstitions, and cures. Even though I was a complete stranger, people showed me around their community, introduced me to their friends, and invited me into their homes. This sort of consideration was shown not only by country people but by "city folk" as well. When I visited the Northeast Archives of Folklore and Oral History, the hospitality of Sandy Ives and his wife Bobby went far beyond the call of duty. When I travelled to the Amos farmhouse in McNairn Settlement, Kent County, I was greeted with a hot cup of tea, a warm supper, and stories that went on non-stop well past midnight. I got up early next morning, and I found Mr. Amos waiting for me with his chair pulled up, his arms folded, and his eyes on the tape recorder. "Plug that thing in," he said, "and let's get going."

Of course there were problems. There was the time I travelled fifty miles, twice, to interview an old fellow who turned out to be mike-shy. "He's hiding in the woodshed," said his wife. But all I got to see was a patch of blue shirt disappearing through the bushes up Porter Cove Brook. And then there was the time the car engine caught fire, sending up ominous billows of smoke. I stood alone on the side of the road in the pouring rain, laden with suitcases, camera, tape recorder, and unsuitably dressed for the occasion. Fortunately I was on the main highway and hailed a bus to get back home.

Another problem was the one I faced when I had to turn the transcriptions from tape into general reading material. My ideal was to tell the tales exactly as they were told. I soon found out it couldn't be done because it was impossible to capture in print the facial expressions, the gestures, and cadence of voice of a master storyteller. Good storytellers will backtrack, digress, and speak in sentence fragments, all of which is natural and entertaining. It adds to the live performance and it sounds great. But if you try to transfer the same thing into print, it doesn't read well. Occasionally I had to interfere with story progression, sentence structures, and phrasing while maintaining the tone, rhythms, speech patterns and, of course, the storyline given by the actual narrator. Wherever possible, I used the speech idioms of the storyteller himself to convey the distinctive poetry of common language.

Some of the stories were told by two people at once (such as the Estey brothers who told "The Red Haired Girl") and other times three or four people told me different anecdotes which centred around one theme, as in the Gorbey story and "The Wizard of Miramichi." I found it awkward to try to maintain more than one or two narrators at once and so I solved the problem by keeping the tone but using my own "voice." I also did this when I adapted stories from a printed source. And so there are a variety of styles here, and perhaps that is as it should be.

It was great fun. I discovered that folklore is not something that occupies a dusty corner in a backroom of the far distant past. It's an ongoing process. Young anglers and hunters still tell tall tales and yarns, and no doubt in the future those stories will be lengthened or widened or changed some way. And, when somebody sees a fireball today, they might not think of "Will o' the Wisp" or "feu follet," but they may believe they have seen a UFO or flying saucer, because the unknown must always be explained, one way or another. That's part of the myth-making process.

True, stories like those told about Geordie Brown come from a bygone age, as do the stories told about other characters like "Snake-eye Jim," who was so long and skinny it took him half an hour to uncoil; or Father Savage of Moncton, who when a fat lady waddled to the front of his church in the middle of mass, said, "We will be silent and wait for the Queen Mary to dock"; or Charlie Cahill of Juniper, who hung a big sign by the highway that read, "SEE THE IRON SPRING," and then lured curious tourists into the woods to see a rusty bedspring hanging from a tree. But, wherever there are characters and topical local events, people will remember them to a certain extent in stories or in songs or in verse. Whenever there is mystery or uncertainty, people will provide their own solutions, especially where none other exists, and ghost stories will be with us for as long as ghosts are seen.

Folklore will be found wherever there are folks.

Elegy for Youth

■ MICHAEL O. NOWLAN
Stubborn Strength: A New Brunswick Anthology, 1983

I remember those trees
great monsters
I could not wrap
my arms around

They were all things
to a small boy—
        a place to swing
                to climb
        or just to rest
on hot summer afternoons

Then government decided
to rebuild
the old dirt road

They came with buzz saws
and cut them all
they even took
the roots

Mother cried

our love is different

■ TROY FULLERTON
Connections, 2008

"our love is different..."
(she thought he was someone else,
the widower.   how queer
it must have been for him,
behind a crowd
of unfamiliar backs
with her,
kissing tasting forgetting).
"natural and eternal"
(she wasn't much for gardening
he kept telling himself as he dug
dug until he hit it.
the lock still warm,
he hammered it off and lifted the lid.
blanket in hand, he crawled inside
tasting her lips, remembering).
...her last words to him.

Fall of '58

WAYNE CURTIS

Preferred Lies: A Collection of Short Stories, 1998

On Friday morning of Thanksgiving weekend, we loaded the truck wagon with provisions enough for three days and left for the lake. Mother made no protest, but before we left she went into the house and slammed the door. The traditional cranberry grounds were across the river and three miles into the woods, through a hundred barrens. Father sat in the front of the wagon on a sack of hay, the stem of his pipe clamped in his teeth, as he drove the horse. I sat facing the back to lessen the horse's smell, as Prince pulled the wagon into the river, still summer-low from the dry season. The wheels bumped and bounced over boulders and we had to stand to keep from being thrown into the water, something we both wanted to avoid as neither of us could swim a stroke. Closer to the lake, the road had grown in with alders and the iron-soled wheels cut into the moss and dropped into ponds, the spokes churning them into mud. Along the way, it started to rain softly, beading the limbs that slapped us, dampening our clothes, yet it remained mild.

At the lake, we tied the horse, covered him with a blanket and pitched our tent on a dry knoll, then assembled a stove pipe and gathered firewood. It was then I began to realize where we were. The North Lake had nothing of the sharp outline I knew as a lake. In fact, it wasn't a lake at all, but another barren with a series of tea-coloured ponds. The remainder of the day we spent wading about the spongy marsh, following the clusters of tangled, transparent vines for the red and purple berries. As it rained harder, a low fog gathered, and at times we could not see one another. By evening we were soaked through.

That night in the tent, I had a toothache. Father dabbed the cavity with kerosene to lessen the pain. The taste of kerosene, the smell of musty canvas, and the stench of the horse were almost choking me. But none of this bothered Father as he sipped his brandy and talked of trips he had made there in the old days, the moose he had shot in the old days, the fun he had had in the old days, the old days, the old days.

Throughout the night, the stove sputtered, protesting the damp wood. It was cold and we didn't manage to get much sleep. Time passed slowly but a reluctant daylight finally emerged through a drab fog and rain as we warmed beans and tea.

At length Father said, "I dare say, I've seen better days. We won't stay much longer, Jimmy." After we had waded in the marsh for a few hours more, he thumbed the face of his pocket watch and mumbled the words I'd been waiting to hear, "Let's get ta hell outta this goddamn moose yard."

On the way home, Father sipped his brandy and sang, in between more of the same stories from the previous night. As the brandy receded in the bottle, the stories became intertwined, like cranberry vines. When he took the wrong road, I grabbed the reins. Father seemed unconcerned as to where we were; he was lost in the old days.

At the river, the horse, sensing danger, refused to wade in. Father cracked the whip and shouted. In a nervous reaction, Prince plunged into the water up to his belly and again Father and I stood on the wagon as I followed the same crossing. But the rain had raised the river. As we reached midstream, the wagon swayed, and when a front wheel ground over a submerged rock, the current pushed the wagon over.

When I emerged from beneath the swirling water I was gasping for breath. My head was aching and I was conscious of a pounding in my chest. I clutched the reins hard, aware that my life depended on their strength. Prince swam, then waded, pulling me by the bit between his teeth. Father grasped the drifting wagon box like death, and, using a plank as an oar, steered to shore. He was bare-headed now, his stringy white hair streaming down his face, but the pipe was still clamped between his teeth. I grabbed his arm and we sloshed to shore, trembling and coughing as the cranberries we had gathered drifted away like so many strings of coloured pearls.

In the kitchen that evening, Father opened his reserve of black rum and drank straight from the bottle. He walked about the room in sock feet and lender top, the bottle in one hand, his pipe in the other. When Mother wasn't looking, he gave me the first drinks of alcohol I can remember tasting. The rum was bitter and it burned my throat and chest and tingled my stomach. He wanted me to play the fiddle for him, so I squeaked out some old tunes, "The Cuckoo's Nest" and "Paddy Whack." When he tried to dance, we both laughed like fools. Father's ringing hearty laugh was a pleasure to hear. I never heard it again. But that night, it seemed that something of the dangerous spirit of his youth survived in him. I remember thinking how he was like he used to be, before he got sick, and I felt something between pride and shame.

Mother remained silent throughout the evening, but in the night she came to my bedroom. The spring squeaked as she sat on my bed. Tugging my shoulder softly, she whispered, "James, are you still awake?"

"Uh-huh."

She sighed heavily.

"I hope you haven't started smoking and drinking," she said with deep concern. When I assured her I hadn't, she said only, "Your father is no example to follow." Tucking the quilts in around me and pausing to touch my face, she returned to her room, down the hall from Father's.

The following morning, Prince stood shivering in the lee of the barn. He was coughing and refused to eat or drink. Father put him in the stable and tried to force-feed him by holding Prince's head and pouring saltpetre into his mouth with a Coke bottle. Nothing worked. He called neighbours who came in groups of three or four, and stood around the barnyard, rolling cigarettes and suggesting remedies. Each had a different diagnosis for the old horse's illness: pneumonia, colic, heaves, black water, and bad grinding teeth were among them. Any of these would be fatal to a horse Prince's age. As the men inspected Prince's hooves, looked in his mouth and under his tail, I could see a sorrow in Father, even though he put a good face on the matter.

"Well, boys, I've been called a long-headed fellah here and there, and I'd say it's the grinders," Father said, trying to hide from his conscience.

"How's he been ta haul?" someone asked.

"He's been good all along," Father argued. To lighten the moment, he added, "There now he couldn't haul a sick whore off a piss-pot!"

"Ha, haaaaaaa! That's a good one!"

"Boys, come way in fer a cup a tea."

In the kitchen, the men broke cookies to dip them in tea and some smoked as Mother pleaded with Father to call the vet. Father wanted no part of this. He said that no long-headed son of a whore from town, who wouldn't know a horse from a jackass, was going to tell him what to do. Besides he and his friends were horse people and knew the practical side of things that a book-learnt man wouldn't. Why should he pay a vet to tell them what they already knew?

"I suppose it's whatever you think, yourself," Mother said. She left the room, knowing she wasn't about to win this argument any more than she won the others, especially not in front of Father's friends.

For the next few days, Father spent more and more time at the barn. Sometimes, he got dressed in the night and went out. I could sense his hopelessness as I watched from my bedroom window as he crossed the dooryard, his pant legs making ghostly shadows in the lantern's glow. I would think, he is not clinging so much to the horse as to a way of life. One night I bundled up and followed after him to the barn. He had the curry comb in one hand and a brush in the other, going over the horse's rump.

"If he's no better by mornin'..." he said.

Later, in bed, I had dreams. I could still feel the strength of the horse, pulling me across the river as I clutched the reins. All night, Father's stories and songs and vignettes of the river incident played like a band of scrambled sounds and images that tangled my mind just above the thinking space. In the early morning I got dressed, rolled a cigarette from Father's tobacco and went out into the dooryard to smoke. It was still raining softly and there was a brown fog that pressed against the buildings. The swollen river, audible from the dooryard, seemed to suggest the gloomy possibility of drowning. I listened for the horse's shuffling in the barn, but there was silence and I prayed that he was dead.

After breakfast I went out to the barn again. I listened, but there was only silence. Opening the door slightly, I peeked in to find Prince staring at me. He gave a deep chuckle and I closed the door, both relieved and disappointed.

Father came out of the house, cradling the thirty-thirty in the crook of his arm. He untied the halter and we led the horse, limping, toward the top hill pasture. As Father walked, he whistled to cover his wheezing. I walked a few yards behind, carrying the gun. As we neared the back edge of the field, Father talked gently to the horse. Then he turned to me and said, "Well, Jimmy, whatta ya think?" and commenced to cough. Father was as pale as a corpse on end, but he did not take a drink that day.

It was warm for November, almost humid, and the heavy fog that hung over the river had lodged the shore grass and buckled the stems of wood brakes. Raindrops were clinging to fir needles and tree trunks and the fence rails were greasy.

Father became militant. He looked at Prince, not as though he were an animal that he had worked with for twenty-five years, but more like he were a strange beast that now stood in his way. I wanted to turn my head, hold my ears and walk from the field. Instead I forced myself to watch, understanding that I had to share this with my father.

He put the gun to the old horse's ear and it barked short in the dampness. There was no echo. The farm seemed to shiver as the horse grunted and dropped to his knees, dark blood spraying from his nostrils. Father fired another shot and the old horse rolled over, his feet in the air. Prince's shoes had been left on for good luck. There was a rank smell of blood and earth and I was vomiting on the grass. My head throbbed and the pasture revolved around me as I clutched the ground and held on.

Father looked at me and I could see the sorrow in him, a sorrow deeper than the despair of this autumn and perhaps closer to that which follows the farewell of a dear woman. It was the first time I had seen this kind of uneasiness in his strained face. As we walked away from the dead horse, he put his hand on my shoulder.

"Well, Jimmy, looks like the rain's about over," he said.

Amanda's Presents, Returned

KATHY MAC
Grain, 2007

Given away to relentless, tail-yanking toddlers, the puppy finally bared fangs
and was sent back. Twelve more years, not one aggressive initiative. Instead,
she ran, hurled her rangy frame out the car door; when the rest of us tumbled

onto the first beach, she'd be a tiny dot exiting the second. A dot that checked in
regularly. Except once, we had to wait, sad figures in a dog-deficient diorama.
I exercised my capacious lungs, and campers behind the second beach learned

her name, her pet names and some less affectionate titles, until enter Amanda,
far right, running like porcupines quilted her heels. The campers' hoorah
fell deafly; too late to share their breakfast bacon, she ignored them, focussed

on my knees, where she crash-landed, joyous and contrite, panting
and in pain. Arthritis. Idiot dog; she'd submerge herself in any flowing
ditch, even mid-winter rimed with ice. Fortunately, glucosamine worked

so well, Elisabeth began taking it for her own aches, and daily ever after
declared "Time for my dog medicine." Her Amanda medicine.

Pride in the Name of Love

PETER T. SMITH
Saint John Telegraph-Journal, August 14, 2007

It's Port City Rainbow Pride Week in Saint John and, yes, "Rainbow Pride" means gay and lesbian pride. And bisexual. And transgender. And, for Aboriginals, two-spirit. It's a pretty inclusive group that will be celebrating diversity this week. Activities include a proclamation from common council, a church service, a dance, a river cruise, and, of course, a parade.

It's also forty years this December since then justice minister Pierre Trudeau, borrowing a phrase from *Globe and Mail* columnist Martin O'Malley, stated, "There's no place for the state in the bedrooms of the nation." Trudeau was referring to legislation he was introducing which decriminalized homosexual activity. Just forty years ago a gay man could be in front of a judge in court for being with his partner. Now he can stand in front of the court clerk and get married to his partner. That's progress.

Some people, with varying degrees of sarcasm, will still ask when there's going to be a straight pride week. The answer is so obvious they can be forgiven for missing it. It's the other fifty-one weeks of the year.

Seriously. It's considered normal, for example, for heterosexuals to show off their wedding rings at work or chat at the office about what you're doing for your anniversary. Many gays and lesbians, however, don't feel enough acceptance to talk freely about their spouses in the workplace. It's awkward, too, because of our inclination to presume everyone's heterosexual.

This must be part of the appeal of Pride Week for gays and lesbians. They can be who they are without having to explain something as personal as their sexuality to casual acquaintances. That and not having to worry about reprisals for being open about who they are. Some heterosexuals (maybe including those wondering about their missing pride weeks) will say they are tolerant but don't want the gays "flaunting it" by talking about their spouses in the same way heterosexuals do.

"Tolerance" seems to have really become a Canadian virtue. But turn that noun into a verb and it doesn't sound quite so nice. "I tolerate you." It's like saying, "You can work here, but don't mention your partner too often." Acceptance, maybe, is a better goal than tolerance, but I doubt that's coming any time soon. On the other hand, it was just a generation ago that we were locking gays up, so maybe in another generation homophobia will firmly take root in its rightful place next to sexism and racism in most people's minds. Of course, we still have a long, long way to go with sexism and racism, too.

The road from tolerance to acceptance seems to be perforated with the potholes of misinformation, hence the bumpy ride. A big question for many people is whether one is essentially "born gay" or it's a matter of choice. Many people wonder about this because they see it as having moral and ethical implications. Anyone who took a first-year psychology course would recognize that as the old "nature versus nurture" debate, and would also remember that any behaviour is the result of multiple causes. Anyone who took such a course in the last ten years would also know that environmental theories of sexual orientation (scientists study "sexual orientation," not "homosexuality") have not been supported by research, whereas the evidence for biological factors continues to mount.

Terminology is another important pothole, because it shapes how we think. "Tolerance" is an example. Another one is "the gay lifestyle." You really never hear many gays and lesbians talking about the "gay lifestyle." That's really something you hear more from people who rarely talk to gays or lesbians. From what I can see, "the gay lifestyle" involves work and careers, parenting and family commitments, and trying to enjoy free time with someone you love. It sounds very much like "the heterosexual lifestyle."

In fact most people, gay and straight, do not prefer to be defined by their sexuality. Those in the public eye, like comedian Rick Mercer, MP Scott Brison, or novelist Ann-Marie MacDonald, quite clearly prefer to define themselves by the quality of their work and their contributions to society. "The gay agenda" (a homosexualized echo of the "world Jewish conspiracy" of yesteryear) similarly doesn't exist, other than perhaps as a general yearning for acceptance and the pursuit of happiness. The closest thing to a gay agenda around here would be at Port City Rainbow Pride's board meeting.

It's pride for the rest of the week in Saint John, and another step towards acceptance in New Brunswick.

Poolside North Conway, NH

DOUG UNDERHILL
River Poems, 2007

Afternoon heavy with humidity
and the smell of apples poolside.
Some dropping to cement and rolling
to water, startling my daughter.

Another hits grass, leaving
leaves shaking. I think of Isaac Newton
and Robert Frost. Science and poetry
meeting. Another muffled thud

as tree lightens. Apples, almost red
as if decorated for Christmas. I pick
one, polish it with hands and shirt,
savour summer's bitter with the sweet.

Along the edge of woods
a deer listens. Hears each apple
drop, waiting for night
to come.

Flying Home

TONY STEELE
Impossible Landscapes, 2005

Flying through the dark
compressed into a chair
you picture the pilots
with their instruments
also flying through the dark.

This experience is well arranged
by others: as if they knew
where you were going to.

You hope you will arrive
at a home familiar and strange.

You approach the airport.
Flaps lower: you feel
an urgency in the dip of a wing.

The window reflects your face
and you see the lights
of the landing strip,

feel the drag of gravity. You say
the names of your children, one by one
I love you, each one of you—
how much? Oh, completely
—as if you will ever know

Feminism and Education in a Flat Earth Perspective

LEO C. FERRARI

McGill Journal of Education, 1975

Limited as we are by the present climate of opinion, the above topic may seem a rather unlikely one. However, most reservations are merely a sign of the lack of evolution in present-day popular thought, which is still engaged in digesting the compatibility of feminism and education. As a result, we still have quite a way to go before both these concepts are seen as relevant to the Planoterrestrialist perspective, which holds to the incontrovertible certitude of the Earth's essential flatness.[1]

It is in the hopes of alleviating somewhat this widespread abysmal ignorance that I address myself to the present topic. I use the adjective "abysmal" advisedly, because the brainwashed mindless majority still refuses to believe in the existence of the Abysmal Chasm, notwithstanding the fact that thousands of people disappear every year without leaving a trace.[2]

Regarding, first, the relevance of the Planoterrestrialist perspective to education, I need only draw attention to one outstanding and utterly incredible phenomenon. Consider the fact that millions upon millions of the members of modern society have been "educated" to the stage where they possess absolute certitude in *not* believing what they see

1. The fraudulent claims for the sphericity of the Earth are exposed, analyzed, and traced to their evil sources in the author's forthcoming book *The Earth is Flat! An Exposé of the Globularist Hoax.*
2. The skeptical reader is referred to John Wallace Spencer's *Limbo of the Lost* (Bantam, 1973) and "The Devil's Triangle" by Marshall Smith (*Cosmopolitan*, September 1973, pp. 198–202).

their own two eyeballs! I am referring of course to the shape of the Earth.[3] Anyone with normal vision can see that the Earth is essentially flat,[4] yet the victims of this strange "education" are incredibly confident that the same Earth is "really" round![5]

This deplorable state of affairs has, of course, been masterminded by those evil Globularists[6] who have succumbed to the mental sickness that the whole Earth is shaped like an incredibly gigantic sphere. These unscrupulous Globularists have surreptitiously instituted a Pavlovian process of conditioning which begins with the newborn and (at that stage) is appropriately entitled "the seduction of the sucklings." By means of round pacifiers, well-rounded routines, round rattles and (later) round balls, an adamantine bondage is established in the infantile mind between the shape of sphericity and social approbation.[7]

At school, the heinous process is continued further with the exposing of the young to those evil-looking globes and mass recitations of that cant: "The earth is round, the earth is round..." Further, more disguised examples of this brainwashing are to be found in such rhymes as "Round and Round the Mulberry Bush," "Humpty Dumpty," and "Sing a Song of Sixpence." Finally, and most significantly, it is to be observed that the aim of the whole educational process is to produce the "well-rounded personality."

Having thus briefly adumbrated the connection (or, more precisely, the lack of connection) between "education" and the Planoterrestrialist perspective, I can only hope that I may have stirred the hearts of some of those involved in this process and perhaps stimulated them to re-examine their approach to education, and particularly to education in regard to the most important topic of

3. "Earth" is consistently capitalized in the author's writings for reasons which will appear.
4. Note the word "essentially" because some simpletons (i.e., Globularists) maintain that Planoterrestrialism teaches that the Earth is as flat as a tabletop. Anyone with the gift of vision can see that the surface of the Earth undulates.
5. As has been well pointed out by the Symposiarch of the Society (Dr. Alden Nowlan), no one is more pitifully foolish than the person who tries to prove by rational argument that the Earth is a sphere (*I'm A Stranger Here Myself*, Toronto: Clarke Irwin, 1974, p. 74).
6. Sometimes referred to as "Globs."
7. Those readers familiar with the Montessori method of education will appreciate only too well the vicious import of this early approach through tactile experiences.

all, namely, the Earth upon which we live. All said and done, there is nothing as important as *terra firma* and (as even the wicked Globularists would agree) the more firmer the less terror.

Next, I would like to address myself to a surprising phenomenon which has been neglected by modern scholars, blinded as they are by Globularistic prejudices. I am referring to the rise of Globularism on the one hand and the decline of archetypal Feminism on the other. Regarding the former, we have only to survey on the grand canvas of history the effects of Globularism upon Man's[8] own self-image. The Great Indignity of sphericizing the Earth has in the long run proven to be but the first step in reducing it to a speck of cosmic dust, and (later) in relegating it to invisibility in some insignificant corner of the supposedly infinite universe. Mankind has accordingly shrunk from its original full-bodied stature through the intermediate stage of being human vermin[9] to the present lamentable stage of being invisible microbes in the supposedly infinite universe. The consequent psychic shock to the human spirit can well be appreciated,[10] if only one can lay aside the Globularistic prejudices and contemplate the effects of the transformation in an objective manner.

In the second place, on the subject of the decline of archetypal Feminism, I am referring basically to the *Untergang* of the Great Mother of the Gods, so viciously attacked by the influential Augustine (among others) in his monumental *City of God*.[11] On the other hand, as that profound French proverb puts it: *comprendre tout, c'est pardonner tout*. The hatred of Augustine and his co-religionists was due in part to the fact that the Bible, upon which they relied so heavily, had already been thoroughly expurgated by a group of misogynists. As Robert Graves has already pointed out in this regard, feminine is the gender that any right-thinking man

8. Unfortunately, the English language does not possess a word corresponding to the German *Mensch* which applies equally to both sexes. However, I trust that the use of "Man" here does not indicate exclusion of the feminine aspect of humanity.
9. Cf. C. S. Lewis's *The Screwtape Letters*.
10. George Sylvester Viereck, *Seven Against Man* (Flanders Hall, 1941), especially pp. 30–31. See also Alexander Koyré's *From the Closed World to the Infinite Universe* (Harper Torchbooks, 1957), especially p. 43, where the author claims that the senseless view of the world created by modern scientific philosophy could lead nowhere else but to nihilism and despair.
11. Augustine, *City of God*, Book 2, chapters 4–5 and 26–27.

would have imputed to the divinity in the first place, for the obvious reason that the divinity is the source of all life and the sustenance of the same.

Now some readers may wonder what this has to do with the Plano-terrestrialist perspective. It has everything to do with it, as I shall attempt to explain briefly hereunder. However, before proceeding to this, it is *à propos* here to dispose of a baseless claim by the Globularists. Some of them claim that making the Earth a sphere (hideous thought!) is favourable to Feminism in that it is adopting a curvaceous conception of terrestrial creation. Well, I hardly need to draw the attention of the more perceptive reader to the scarcely latent sexism in that baseless claim. Further, the staunch champion of Common Sense, George Bernard Shaw, has rightly taken Newton (the chief theoretician of the Globularists) to task for inflicting upon posterity (without so much as asking its permission) the very opposite of a curvaceous conception of creation.[12] Newton's nonsense[13] vainly postulates a rectilinear universe in which curves are barely tolerated as unfortunate anomalies.[14]

Regarding next the connection between the decline of the Great Mother and the rise of Globularism, it is of fundamental import to realize that the Mother is none else but our beloved Earth upon whom we all live and move and have our being.[15] As Pliny has so beautifully described, "She it is who gives birth to us, nourishes and supports us through life and when all our fellow beings reject us in the end, it is She again who receives us back into her Bosom."[16]

Once this key concept is grasped, a sudden sense springs into

12. Recall Newton's basic principle that every body will move forever in a *straight line*, unless compelled by an external force to change that (highly hypothetical) state.
13. The word "nonsense" is used advisedly here, in view of the highly suspicious circumstances surrounding the "discovery" of the "Law" which held the universe (i.e., Newton's universe) together. This has been well pointed out by the Chancellor of the Flat Earth Society, H.R.H. James Stewart, in his tractate "Newton?—Nonsense!" As we know from Voltaire (who had the details from a cousin of Newton's), he (i.e., Newton) was one day sitting under an apple tree, when he found his thoughts profoundly moved by the fall of an apple. It would appear that this unfortunate man had the temerity to pronounce upon the nature of the universe after having been struck on the head by a falling object.
14. Witnessed, in the present context, by the supposed elliptical paths of planets around the sun.
15. Cf. *Acts* 17:28.
16. Pliny, *Natural History*, 2.63.154. Cf. Sirach 40.1.

the history of Western cosmology. Globularism is seen for what it is—the first step in a vicious and sustained belittling of the Earth, which would transform Her from the Pillar and Ground of our Being to some invisible speck of dust lost in an infinite universe. In its turn, this revolt against the Great Mother has begotten such monstrous manifestations of attempted escape from Her as mechanized flight (real or simulated), concentrated centres of population together with hideous skyscrapers (thereby minimizing contact with Her), illusions of "space flight,"[17] and last, but not least, the boast of being able to blow the very Earth Herself into a trillion pieces. These and many other similar phenomena are nothing else but the symptomatic manifestations of a profound and debilitating *terraphobia*,[18] which is now seen to be the mainspring of the centuries of rationalizing initiated by the Globular perspective.[19]

In conclusion, therefore, I trust that even so brief an outline has given some idea of the Planoterrestrialist perspective as vitally necessary to a sane apprehension of reality whereby the eye of the heart and the eye of the mind can be brought into focus with each other. Too, it can perhaps be appreciated that Planoterrestrialism constitutes the very Ground of true Feminism. I trust therefore that the importance of the Planoterrestrialist perspective to education is somewhat better appreciated.

---

17. Another of the fabrications of a government which has been shown to have been riddled with corruption. It is also noteworthy that the name "astronaut" is a very pretentious title indeed, since its possessors had nothing to do with stars. They supposedly committed the grossest of obscenities of treading upon the very face of the moon. If anything, they should be termed "lunanauts."
18. This fear of the Earth is manifested in the fact that Dirt has now assumed the social detestation accorded to Satan in the Middle Ages. As a result, vast armies of grim housewives see their raison d'être as willing combatants in the Great War against Dirt, a phenomenon which posterity will probably find as intriguing as the Crusades of medieval Christendom.
19. In regard to the attempted flight from the Great Mother, it is noteworthy that the most pernicious of the astronomical theories to come out of the Renaissance were deeply rooted in the medieval conception of abstraction. Observe, too, the very definition of this process: *per abstractionem fit separatio a materia*. In view of previous considerations, it can be appreciated that the orthography of this definition is *per abstractionem fit separatio a matre*. Whence—behold: *materia—mater—madre—Mutter—Mother* [sic]! In other words, the whole process is motivated by the desperate desire to escape from the Great Mother—that is, from the Earth itself, a feat which the present age has vainly set itself as a goal to be accomplished in the physical sense, even if by blowing the whole Earth to pieces, as a last resort.

On taking down an elm

ANDREW TITUS
Fiddlehead, 2006

First, you must ask for
giveness and have
        soothing words concerning health
        of the pack, and holy descriptions
incanting gravity, and the horizon.

This will at least
prepare twigs for snapping and
trunk for land.

                Next, kneel
near the roots and
        humming

recite stories of civilization's rise
from volcanic outpourings, and of
the fall—how it hurts

only for a second.

Reinventing Darkness

■ EDWARD GATES
Heart's Cupboard, 2006

when the guest leaves there
is never enough light left

my cup runneth over   the harvest returns
old leaves swirl new life into the ground

desire holds and the cluster of bees
follows the honey stored in the hive

be patient sisters   it took
fourteen years to cure this wine

the final solution   the cutting of old
ties   a dry spring for a heavy load

The Man from Murphysboro

:: DAN GLEASON
Nashwaak Review, 1995

I never thought my father would die in a nursing home, but he did. On the first Tuesday of December, just as my mother had almost exactly three years before. They had been married for over fifty years, he the breadwinner, she the housewife-mother-money manager. My mother's death left him alone for the first time since 1939, but he readapted to single life well. He did his laundry, cooked for himself, kept the house clean, shopped, paid the bills, and so on. His neighbours, old workmates, and friends in St. Andrew's Parish supported him, and he spent most of his free time working on projects and activities of the Knights of Columbus.

They were from St. Louis (my sister and I were born there) and had moved to Murphysboro, population ten thousand, in southern Illinois in 1949. My dad, who had not finished high school, had learned his trade, printing, in various printing plants in St. Louis. He grabbed the opportunity to be a superintendent in a new rotogravure plant. Gradually, they made their lives in Murphysboro, raising a family, making friends, working, and participating in the life of the small town. There were still trips back to St. Louis, either on the Illinois Central or Gulf Mobile and Ohio railroads or, later, once my dad learned to drive, in the family car.

Murphysboro was a bustling little town in the 1950s. Besides the printing plant, there was a shoe factory. All told, it had some nine hundred industrial jobs. We grew up with the shoe factory whistle serving to signal us home for homework and supper. Somehow, its population has never grown beyond ten thousand. The shoe factory closed down, as most shoe factories in the United States have long since succumbed to globalization. The railroads no longer stop in Murphysboro, as most railroad lines have long since been terminated. The town's main street records the decline of Murphysboro, with once-gracious homes converted to stores that have long since gone out of business, with gaping spaces where burnt-out stores were never replaced. Most people prefer to shop in the Carbondale shopping mall, only seven miles away. Like so many other small towns, Murphysboro has seen its young move away in search of careers.

To an outsider such as I am now, life in my old home town seems to border on the desperate. But it wasn't so when I was growing up there. Children are too distracted by the immediacy of life to consider the larger perspective. We accepted the world of the 1950s through the filter of small town life and didn't worry about the larger issues of the day. Now, having gone back there for my father's funeral, I look back on that time and place in a different light.

What strikes me now is how alive and well racism was in Illinois, "The Land of Lincoln," as licence plates remind us. The grade schools were segregated. Catholic children attended St. Andrew's; other white kids went to Lincoln or Washington grade schools and Logan Junior High. The "coloured," when we weren't calling them something else, had their own grade school, Douglass, after the ex-slave abolitionist, Frederick Douglass. We never played with coloured children, even though the black part of town was adjacent to our school playground. Our basketball and softball teams never played against theirs. Of course, there was an unofficial colour line regarding residential and employment patterns. The coloured lived within their section on the extreme edge of town next to the Big Muddy River. They were not generally seen outside of that area. They did not work in the shoe factory or the printing plant. The movie theatre had a balcony in which there was a four-foot high barrier. The coloured sat only in the balcony and on their side of the divider. They reached that seating area by their own stairway.

Whites had their own stairway to their side of the balcony. One of the railroads had separate cars for whites and the coloured.

And all of this took place north of the Mason-Dixon Line. We lived in Illinois, not Alabama, and it all seemed normal to us. Perhaps this is not so surprising. Illinois has the shape of a hand on a north-south axis, with the finger tips extending southward between the Mississippi and Ohio rivers. Southern Illinois, settled by people moving westward from Kentucky (such as Abraham Lincoln's family), is located south of a line stretched between St. Louis and Louisville. It is flanked by Missouri and Kentucky, once slave states. Attitudes and folkways were Southern and remained so for a century after the Civil War.

That has all changed now, at least outwardly so. To a large extent, economic depression has obviated the possibility of segregation. There is no Douglass School, no railroad, no shoe factory. The movie theatre was demolished and never replaced. Blacks may reside on any street in Murphysboro, although the old coloured part of town is still predominantly Black.

My father had never thought that he would die in a nursing home. And it didn't seem very likely that he would. He was too strong for that. He had started jogging in the 1960s, long before that activity became popular. Later, after he retired, he ran competitively in five- and ten-kilometre races, usually bringing home a trophy for first or second place in the over-sixty or over-seventy age categories. He ran in races all over southern Illinois, in St. Louis, and as far away as Colorado. Trophies, plaques, coffee mugs, and T-shirts—mementoes of the hundreds of races that he entered—cluttered the TV room, closets, and the basement of his house. St. Andrew's Parish even named the 5K run of its annual festival in his honour. Townspeople knew him for his daily runs of three to four miles. All this until his late seventies, when he was struck by prostate cancer. Thereafter, he had to limit himself to walking and officiating races.

My father would rather have been in Murphysboro than any other place on earth. He had made his connections there. People knew him and hailed him. Although he was not a verbal person, he was interested in people. That was his way. His sister Betty told of one of his grade school teachers, a nun, who said of him, "He doesn't care what I say, but he knows every ragpicker who comes down the alley." He had the gift of laughter. He was generous and helpful, giving of his time and energy to friends and volunteer work. The people who worked for him consistently remarked on his tactfulness and consideration. So when he visited us, wherever we lived, Washington, DC, Puerto Rico, Notre Dame, Berkeley, or Fredericton, he was always more interested in getting back to Murphysboro than he was in any diversions we had planned. A place that had come to seem depressed and desperate to me was beautiful to him because of his involvements with the people there. Murphysboro was not a dying town to him; it was his place, where he and his buddies at the KC ran the weekly bingo, where he served Meals on Wheels, where he watched the high school athletic events, where his neighbours watched out for him and he for them.

Because he was strong, I never thought he would die in a nursing home. But only a few days after he moved into the Jackson County Nursing Home, it became clear to him that he would never leave it. One memory haunts me. We were alone in his drab, overheated room, when he asked me if he would someday be able to return to his own home. I told him directly, without dint of tact, "No, you will not leave here." Then I tried to recover, explaining that I would not lie to him. Since then I have tried to reconcile myself to the argument that I did the right thing, that I treated him with dignity by telling him the bald truth. But there was no hiding the implication of my unequivocal answer.

He had bone cancer and it could not be reversed. Once the cancer took hold, his strength deteriorated quickly. My sister had visited him in October and had detected no alarming health problems. She noted that he had slowed down, but that was understandable for a man of his age. Then, in the last eight weeks, the cancer began to spread. His friends, even the nurses, said it was good that he didn't suffer too long. I accept that. But he did suffer.

By the time my sister and I reached him, ten days before his death, he had just been transferred from the Murphysboro hospital to the nursing home. Initially, he expected to regain strength and go home. At first, we walked the halls with him, very slowly and not very far, maybe the equivalent of two city blocks. He was uncomfortable, his feet were swollen, but he still had an appetite. His decline was precipitous. Within days he could no longer walk, not even the ten feet to his bathroom. I had to help him in and out of bed. Disgusted, he said, "How helpless can I be." The cancer was consuming him from within. He spit up blood, lost the strength to eat, lost weight. His skin was jaundiced and splotched by subcutaneous bleeding. His breath grew frighteningly faint. As fluid accumulated in his lungs, he developed a rattle. And he could not sleep. The day before he died, he told a hospice worker that anxiety about death kept him awake nights.

My father was stoic. He preferred not to bother others. He had a high threshold of pain, but on his last day he asked for more painkillers. A nurse told him that he already had been given his limit. I have this: I told him that I loved him before I left that morning. He died that afternoon. An orderly found him. He had just stopping breathing.

His death was a deliverance. His priest had visited him, prayed with him, anointed him. For me, it brought tremendous, immediate relief.

[Je pense aux livres...]

■ PAUL CHANEL MALENFANT
Des ombres portées, 2000

Je pense aux livres que j'ai lus dans ton dos.

J'ai déposé sur ta pierre un panier d'impatiences.
Elles souffrent l'ombre.

Nous n'avons pas vu venir le noir.
Ni les voyelles étrangler les sanglots dans nos gorges.

Et cette couleur, *sépia*,
nous paraissait d'un autre temps.
D'un autre monde.

Alors j'écris : *Cendres, dédicaces.*

[I think about the books . . .]

:: Translation by MARYLEA MacDONALD
If This Were Death, 2009

I think about the books I read over your shoulder.

I placed on your stone a basket of impatiens.
They can bear the shade.

We did not see the darkness coming.
Nor the vowels strangle the sobs in our throats.

And that colour, *sepia*,
Seemed to come from another time.
From another world.

So I write: *Ashes*, *dedications*.

Automatic Garage Door Opener

GARY J. LANGGUTH
Schrodinger's Cat, 1996

The wife swears by the Murphy-brand automatic garage door opener. She says "Thank God for the one Junior installed for the daughter." Billy passed away last summer—just full of cancer—and the daughter hit the bottle again. She couldn't handle being alone up there in old Thelma's trailer. New Year's Eve, she put gas in Billy's Ford truck, backed into the garage, wrote a note, and turned on the motor. She hit the automatic garage door opener, but didn't the damn thing jam halfway down. Those things are a fifty-dollar piece of shit, but the daughter is in treatment and the wife has bought five more openers as birthday gifts.

Of Particle and Wave

NORMA JEAN PROFITT
Journal of Progressive Human Services, 2003

How do I speak of my relationship with the country of Costa Rica and the friends that I have there? Where do I begin and how do I describe what has happened to me without sounding banal, as if nothing of significance has occurred, as if nothing has altered the cells of my body and the face that I wear? How do I capture in paragraphs of letters and words the *duelo* (mourning) that I have lived for over a decade? And how do I transmit where I have come to now, with all that I did not leave behind? The English language alone does not render the words I need.

I left for Costa Rica in 1987 to work with CUSO, a Canadian non-governmental international development organization. During my five years there, I worked with two women's organizations. The first, a rural women's organization based in the town of San Ramón, was just beginning to daringly raise the issue of men's violence against women in its communities, and the second, a feminist collective with headquarters in the capital city of San José, was dedicated to community organizing and education with poor women in urban and rural communities. Of my arrival in Costa Rica that first time, I recall the gentle roundness of the lush mountains as we descended into the airport Juan Santamaría and my *presentimiento* (presentiment) that I would be radically altered by my life here. The sensation of the warm air against my skin as I emerged from the airport into the late afternoon of a Costa Rican early summer returns to calm me with its caress whenever I summon that memory. That evening, after I had settled into my room in the home of the family where I was staying while I attended language school, Susan, a co-operant with a British organization, came to get me and we went for a stroll in the village of San Antonio de Belen. Of that day I remember most of all the exact insistence of the breeze as it touched my face and the diffuse fragrance of the tropical flowers in the night air. How could there be such beauty? We walked for some time and I went home to sleep, exhausted and exhilarated. I was bewitched.

If explanations are called for, I cannot say how I merged so readily into the flowers, the climate, the landscape, the aliveness of that world. I only know that I spent much time in nature walking long distances in the rainy season downpours, often to a friend's house in the country, exploring the vegetation and fauna, and admiring and painting in watercolours the flowers that graced the everyday. I have always thought about my relationship with nature as a way of living in one of the otherworlds. As a child the only other person I knew who inhabited these otherworlds was my grandmother, always imperceptibly connected to other realms, one of these being nature: the sunsets, the gladioli, the trees, the dew, the birdsong, the sway of the barley, the spring violets so tiny and precious, the red of the Cortlands, the smell of the apple blossoms, the silkiness of rabbit's fur, the texture of a hen's egg. And perhaps like her, I too live in that otherworld a good deal of the time, saving myself for what I can know in my body, in my skin.

Although I am ashamed to admit it, I carried to Costa Rica the discourse of "helping," a racist discourse well grounded in the whiteness and privilege that permeates "developed" countries. Such a narrative establishes inhabitants of "undeveloped" countries as *los atrasados* (the backward) who require "help." Without exactly knowing, but no doubt fired by unconscious investment, the unspoken word power of this discourse shaped my relations with Costa Rican women. I felt this shaping much more than I saw it. As I unearthed my assumptions about what I could contribute as a co-operant, this notion of helping turned hollow and absurd. I swung to the other end of the spectrum then—what did I have to contribute after all? Like many *extranjeros* (foreigners) who visit, live, and work in Costa Rica, would I end up consuming the women in my desire to know them? Would I be one of those who devours the Other without taking the risk of being known? I struggled with how to dismantle those chains that chafed from the inside and from the out. As I took up what is called in Costa Rica *un proceso de acompañamiento* (a process of accompaniment), I became more comfortable with my place in the work, and more able, with *compañeras* (comrades), to challenge the play of oppressive power in our daily encounters.

In San Ramón I became friends with two women involved in the rural women's organization, *Mujeres Unidas en Salud y Desarrollo* —MUSADE (Women United in Health and Development). Adita was then a member of MUSADE and a community leader. Ligia was then a community nurse with the Ministry of Health and an *asesora* (advisor) to MUSADE. Through these friendships, the categories that are constructed about us, that construct us, and that we construct about each other, slowly fell apart. What is a Canadian? Who was I as *la canadiense* (the Canadian)? And what did *costarricense* (Costa Rican) tell me about Adita and Ligia? Yet they are, I am, we are all entangled with country as place, as we are with language and culture. How can we separate our friendship from place, from our lives there? I thought about the purpose of all those clichés about "getting to know people for who they are," "seeing the person first," "realizing that underneath it all we're really the same." They failed desperately to capture the process and the friendships themselves—the intents, the tentative reachings, the lulls, the revealings, the enormity of oscillating between many worlds, our internal (*cada cabeza es un mundo*: each person's head is an entire world) and our social and cultural worlds. How did we move through fear and the likelihood that I might be one of those who came to exploit? How was I "one of us," as Adita said to me, "*usted es de nosotros, del pueblo, no de esos explotadores*" ("you are one of us, of the people, not one of those exploiters")? What did that mean to her, to me, that I was one of us, but yet, I could come to Costa Rica and go back to Canada, always a sign of privilege?

After two and one-half years in the rural area, I went to work with *el Colectivo de Mujeres Pancha Carrasco* (the Women's Collective Pancha Carrasco), a feminist collective in San José, the capital of Costa Rica. I became friends with a woman, Dellanira, who was born and raised in Tabasco, México, and moved to Costa Rica fourteen years ago. We worked together on the *Equipo de Identidad de Género* (Gender Identity Team) and in a small semi-rural community working with women who formed a mutual support group to confront men's violence against them. What brought us together then was our mutual desire to understand our lives as women, brown and white, the oppression of our souls that we had experienced in our families, the sources of sustenance that sparked our rebellion and moved us toward life. We read feminist texts, opened ourselves to emotions, and put words to many happenings in our lives about which we had never before spoken. I had never felt as if I belonged anywhere, particularly in the work realm, but this experience was for me the closest I have ever come to what I imagine belonging to be — to be comfortable in a place, challenged firmly but gently, and to feel wanted, accepted, and understood.

What is it about an environment that invites us to be something more than what we have been, to say yes, *sí*, I will. What is the nature of the *ánimo*, the spirit, that lies in wait, anticipating? And who had I been before I came to Costa Rica and what was I becoming now? I gave myself up to be seen, to be known, I, who had grown up to conceal myself. And who was I, who were we to risk loving, loving in a short time, I, who always waited for guarantees to love? How was it that I could love these friends with a fierceness, a *ferocidad*, I who was terrified of loss of any kind? What was it about the place and the people that forged my desire to live and love, when I had done it so poorly before? I am still surprised that I was able to be there, present, in my skin.

I returned to live in Canada in May of 1992, ten years ago now. I came back to do a doctorate degree at Wilfrid Laurier University, in Waterloo, Ontario. It was a second choice after realizing that I did not have the financial means to study in Latin America. But somewhere in the recesses of my mind I ask myself if I had been determined, could I not have found a way to stay? I experience it now as a failure, a failure of nerve. In that decision-making process I remember the recurring tugs on *mi alma* (my soul): *quédese, no se vaya* (stay here, don't go). The disquiet that I felt then resurfaces, hovers, and waits to be named. Can I dare to say it, that I feared a falling, a tumbling into, a drifting too far away? In a place where I had experienced connection and belonging, how could I have been afraid of becoming unmoored? What I mean is this: to have become more untethered from a kind of security, from my privilege and identity, would have signalled the impossibility of a return to what was, at least, familiar. How strange that I held back, when in actuality that possibility of return had already been closed off. And therein lies the betrayal and the question still within: if I had unleashed myself, where would I be now? What could I have become?

I do not remember much about the immediate years after the return, except for the *sollozos* (sobs) that would erupt suddenly, only to spend themselves and spin into depression. In the beginning I tried to explain to friends what my life had been like there and how I had felt, but they could not grasp the essence of my experience. I suspect that my inept efforts at description were shrugged off as romanticism or self-deception. I began to worry that I was using some form of delusionary as a salve to ease the pain. But if so, it did not work, but rather sharpened it. Occasionally, I talked with a friend from Costa Rica who had also been a co-operant with CUSO. We lamented that we had felt so alive, so close to the bone. She was the only person who truly understood what I was experiencing, but she lived far away. I berated myself: why couldn't I feel that here, that intensity, that vigour, that connection? Much later I realized that my bonds with friends and nature lay fertile beneath my skin, in *el calor de fértil tierra* (the heat of the fertile earth).[1] It was their loss I lived through my body, flailing about in impotent rage, desperately seeking traces of *ánimo*.

At the same time that I was depressed, I railed against everything and everyone, criticizing capitalism and the *tonterías* (foolishness)

1. *"Calor de fértil tierra"* comes from a poem that Dellanira Pérez Naranjo wrote for me when I left Costa Rica in 1992. *"Llevarás entre piel este color, calor de fértil tierra"* (You will carry beneath your skin this colour, heat of the fertile earth.)

of the Canadian people as if they were a monolithic whole, for their materialism and staidness. As an outsider in my PhD program, I rebelled against the university system with its rules and inflexibility, its refusal to recognize life experience, its disdain of emotion, its uniformity and blandness. To induce the feeling of being in Costa Rica, I pasted photographs of the trees, flowers, grasslands, and beaches on my walls. Bodily, I could recall the soft rain falling against my skin, the smell of the *jazmín de la noche* (jasmine of the night), the satiny touch of the blood red *amapola* (poppy) that I painted. But at the same time that I grieved, I could not often pick up a pen to write or the telephone to call. I knew then that I was too *dolida* (tender) and I thought that I would break apart, come undone.

To describe what I felt over the years is difficult because I can only find words that do not yield the meaning I need to convey. A physical presence of an absence, an ache perhaps, a reminder of what isn't, a desire that is both desire and its lack. After listening to me lament, some people said to me, "Ah, but you'll adjust, you'll get over it." Get over what, precisely? How strange to think that an experience so formative could be gotten over. What could that mean? How do you get over joy, friendship, and loss when they have become part of you, as if somehow coming to terms with and letting go was all that was required to move on, to bring that word that I so detest—closure. Rather the opposite, that mourning grief is a process of integration, of distilling, of holding on and holding dear, of desiring, of re-encountering, of reclaiming that part of me that the people and the place called forth, that with time became more insistent, *más conspicuo por su ausencia* (more conspicuous because of its absence). *Una bendición* (a blessing).

I have returned to Costa Rica five times since 1992. On my most recent visits, I felt as if I never left. I regain my command of the language and am immersed in it, dreaming in it, living it as part of me. The friendships that mattered to me have deepened in ways that I could not have imagined. Yes, the country, the place has changed, but so have we, in different ways. But to love across distance, to see each other and be known, is the fruit of our friendship. The spirit with which my friends live seems better equipped to deal with the *encuentros, reencuentros, y partidas* (encounters, re-encounters, and departures); I futilely resist that meetings, separations, and the *paréntesis* (parentheses) in between are inevitable.

In being with friends, reminiscing and reflecting, I realized that I have grown from the slow burn of missing them. The folds and layers that connect us so delicately are marbled through us in the presence of the other. For me, given my history and the hopes and fears that I have struggled with all my life, the joy of again being able to express feelings without censure, to say yes, I will miss you, I am sad, I am suffering, I am so content, I am enraged—is a blessing. Every day now I struggle to hold on to that *ánimo* and to brave the times when it escapes me, when it threatens to evaporate and does, only to sleep until I call it back, again and again.

I live in two worlds, here and there, and in the between space, here not fully alive and there quivering. Remembering, the feelings of being bound in this place fall away; the moment is. What is the nature of that *ánimo* that dissipates within days of returning from Costa Rica? How could I not be *de luto* (in mourning)? That I could love despite my *partida* (departure), not knowing when or if I might see my beloved friends and land, has brought a sharpness, a clarity about the richness and tenuousness of connection. I used to worry about the sustainability of such long-distance friendships, but this no longer preoccupies me, for they are forged in fondness, shared experience, accompaniment, and tears, and they too can disappear.

How can a place both catalyze a dormant internal process and graciously proffer the conditions in which to remould early formative experiences? How could it be that I was blessed with the chance to retrieve the submerged and mend the disconnections in my past, pulling these threads into the present? Was it because I lived more in my body than I had ever done before? Was it the tropical climate and closeness to nature that encouraged more living in my cells? Why was I able to be more vulnerable to others, to let them see my tenderness when here I have so often felt so closed and so hard? I fear that I replicate the discourse of the oppressor. Haven't we all heard it before? White, "First World," privileged people who have lived in "Third World" countries saying that our experience there allowed us to live pieces of ourselves that we could not own in our native country? Isn't that what we always do, suck the life out of wherever we go, *como parásitos* (like parasites), and leaving *cuando nos da la gana* (whenever we feel like it).

Is something else never possible? Yes, it is. Yet the presence of caring, love, *voluntad* (will), critical self-consciousness, a commitment to social justice are not enough. They cannot guarantee that we navigate toward a different kind of relationship. My own desire was an amalgam of longing, faith, and fear. If I could touch its core, I would say that it was a burning presence that exacted from me, in relationship with others, a falling back hard upon myself and a going beyond my borderlines.

I was born into a culture and a language; I have a language and a place but they only partially have me. Why does listening to the Spanish language reach into me deeper than English, my mother tongue, could ever do? Why is every word part of the larger story? The language of English does not rivet me to every word, to the subtlety of pronunciation, to the laughter inside, to the pain that a word intends to carry; it does not captivate me nor hold me in its bubble, riding, waiting, bursting, expectant until the next breath. Does the Spanish language itself capture the life force more completely? Did this tongue alter the angle with which I met time? I remember many occasions, and most recently on my visit, when it seemed as if time opened up into a timelessness, a vastness, to illuminate a slice of our momentary existence, yet with the accompanying knowing that it matters immensely how we live our lives. All of this was part of what split me open.

My life in Costa Rica, and all that has flowed from it, changed my way of thinking about our lives, of being with people. Yes, my experience there strengthened some of the values I held, and more importantly, shifted the balance and borders of my worldview. My work with colleagues and with women in the communities connected me with their strengths, desires, and vulnerabilities, and reconnected me with my own. The challenge to be with them in their wholeness repaired the rifts in my own person. My experience of accompaniment encouraged a quality of self-reflection in the spirit of collective and personal growth, and a degree of self-honesty couched in acceptance from which I did not flinch as much. It nourished compassion and solidarity with others and toward my own self, and fostered more acceptance of uncertainty, change, possibility, and hope. And I have come to know viscerally that solidarity is a placing there, a calling into, an act of recognition, and *un compromiso consigo mismo* (a commitment to oneself).

Mi experiencia en Costa Rica me ha permitido experimentar tantas cosas, tantos sentimientos—el sentirme viva, el amor a vida, la alegría, la ternura, la amistad, la vulnerabilidad, la lealtad, y la gratitud. En el proceso del abrirme a la otra, a las otras, me comprometí a revelar mi propia complicidad. Lo que me ha quedado es este compromiso conmigo misma, el cual significa a la vez un compromiso a la reciprocidad. Nuestra creación de un espacio fecundo nos lleva a una política cotidiana subversiva y a la resistencia colectiva contra la injusticia. (My experience in Costa Rica has allowed me to experience so many things, so many feelings—the feeling of being alive, the love of life, joy, tenderness, friendship, vulnerability, loyalty, and gratitude. In the process of opening myself up to the other, to others, I made a commitment to myself to uncover my own complicity. What has remained with me is this engagement which is, at the same time, a commitment to reciprocity. Our creation of a fertile space in which to encounter each other carries us to a daily, subversive politics and a collective resistance against injustice.)

November

■ VERNON MOOERS
Nashwaak Review, 1998

The day after this Halloween Lily phones.
She wants to go up one more time to see the lake—
the leaves turning orange to brown
and the five loons swimming, oblivious.
My grandmother is ninety-one and a half.
She wants to clean the fridge out
check on things
make sure the cottage will make it through winter
last one more season
says her daughter in Calgary wants to keep it,
some crazy idea about spending summers there
  she laughs.

I have better things to do
so I hike the ski-doo trail
back up through swamp to the apple orchard
find the partridge feeding there
five of them, filling their crops,
stretched skin beneath feathered fur,
expecting seeds and cedar buds will help them make it
through another hard, cold winter.
But I am a murderer, shoot three of them
for a fistful of meat

and one cries out in pain,
suffering as they are prone to.
And I walk the trail back down
the meat still warm against my back,
stuffed in the game pocket in the wool
of my great-grandfather's hunting jacket.

And we leave the cottage to the mice and bats
the garden to foraging rabbits, squirrels and porcupines.
And one lone young duck down by the shore
plays in the water
sits unheeding with his silly daffy grin.
He better get moving south too,
or he won't get there at all.
I know next week this lake will freeze
just as it always does,
for one season more.

edmund somebody

FREDERICK MUNDLE
Contemporary Verse 2, 1997

as he curved forward toward his room
he looked like an old question mark

asking his way with his forgetful slippers
then his head bobbed up higher

than his dowager's hump in answer
to finding his door   with the knuckle

of his forefinger he tapped a yellow memo
sheet on the doorframe with his name printed on it

my room   he said proudly   as his half empty blue eyes rolled
up to it   looking as though he were speeding in slow motion

he became a question mark again asking
the dark where his bed was   and seemingly asking

the long night to be patient
as he had half a mind not to die just yet

Up in the Air and Down

■ LORNA DREW
Fiddlehead, 2007

When the city cut down the big elm in front of her house, Moira didn't watch. She stayed in her room with the door shut and her fingers in her ears, feeling as though her own limbs were being severed. So painful, she thought. I'm sure it's screaming. Can trees scream?

When it was over, and they'd dragged the trunk and branches off, she still refused to look at the stump. She walked past it, head averted, on her way to the grocery store. Bill, her neighbour, was out watering his garden.

"Pity about that old tree," he said. "It had real character. The house looks different without it."

"Yes, well, Dutch elm disease. Nothing else to be done." Still avoiding eye contact with the stump, Moira walked on. She knew she'd sounded abrupt. She couldn't help it. She couldn't discuss that tree with anyone. Not yet. Once she and Ed had hung a swing for the kids on one huge, gnarled branch. And one night, unable to sleep, they'd gone out in their pajamas and swung on it themselves, shushing each other and giggling. Ed stood on the seat and pumped them into the stars. Up in the air and down. It was wonderful. They'd come in and made love. Ed. The old tree carried his imprint. She should have had it cremated and kept its ashes along with Ed's. Stupid to think of it now. Let it go. It was just a tree.

But she still didn't feel right. Like mourning again but with no finality. No closure. She hated that term. Hated everything new now. Why did things have to change? Language should stay the same. So should trees. Things changed but they didn't get better. Like bread machines, she thought the next day, punching down dough. I should get a bread machine. I could save a lot of time. And what would I do with the time I saved with Ed dead and the kids gone? I'm just another old woman alone. Nothing to do and no one to do it with.

On the third day she was out of butter and she had to go to the store. This time she made herself look. Forced her gaze to settle on the stump where it stayed riveted while her heart beat too fast and her knees trembled. On the stump was the imprint of a face. In the rings and whorls marking the old tree's genealogy, she could see a man's face quite clearly. It was a thin face, with large, gentle eyes, lines down both sides of a long, straight nose and full, sensuous lips curved in a slight smile. "Hello, Ed," said Moira. Then she sat down and cried.

She was still there, sitting on the grass in tears, when Lois came over. "I saw you out my window. What are you doing?" I'm sitting on the grass crying in front of a tree stump, Moira thought. It's my grass and my stump and I'm old enough to do as I like on my own property. But Lois was a nice woman, even though she was married to Bill.

"Look at the tree, Lois. Who does that look like to you?"

But Lois was not only looking at the tree, she was on her knees in front of it, and her hands were raised and her mouth was moving. Silly woman, thought Moira perversely, watching her neighbour. It's only Ed. She's seen him before.

"It's okay, Lois, it startled me at first, but it's just Ed. I mean it's the sort of thing he'd do to be funny and here I am crying over it. I'm sure it was supposed to be a joke. We might as well get up. I was just going to the store. Would you like some tea?"

When Lois didn't move, Moira moved closer. "Bless me, Father," Moira could hear her saying, "for I have sinned," but she wasn't talking to Moira. She was talking to Ed in the stump. If he blesses her, Moira thought, bustling next door to find Bill, she'll be some surprised.

She found Bill fixing the lawn mower and explained things to him. "Ed's face is in the tree stump, Bill, and Moira's praying to it. Could you come?" She knew it sounded funny but Bill, for a change, didn't question her. He wiped his hands and came. She pointed out Lois, still praying or something, and the next thing she knew there were two of them, Bill and Lois both, on their knees in the grass worshipping Ed. She couldn't figure it out. Lois was a churchgoer but Bill, as far as she knew, hadn't gone to church in years. She guessed that's what happened when you'd been alone for a while. You lost touch with the neighbours. "Bill." He turned from the stump and saw her. "Christ, Moira. It's Christ. You've got some kind of miracle here. You better phone the police."

Just like Bill to want to bring in the authorities. He'd always been bossy, even in school. And besides, why would she want the police around, staring at Ed? It wasn't illegal, was it, to turn up in a tree? He wasn't harming anyone. Did Bill say Christ? "Did you say Christ, Bill? That's just Ed. That's just the way he used to look at me. I ought to know my own husband."

Bill looked at her curiously. "That's Christ, Moira. Just like in his pictures. Ever see the shroud of Turin? That's the image, right there. That's his face, except for the smile. Look at the eyes. I'm calling the press. We shouldn't fool around with this. We've been chosen. We've got to act responsibly." He turned to Lois. "I'm calling the papers, dear. I'll be back." Lois didn't move. "Would you like tea?" Moira said again to her neighbour and, hearing no reply, went in to make a pot.

She made the tea with leaves, not bags, carried the pot to the kettle, and steeped it for five minutes. Then she sliced some fresh cheese bread, buttered it, put it on a china platter with sugar, lemon and three cups, and carried it out to the lawn. There were four people on her lawn now. Three passersby had joined Lois, still on her knees but no longer praying. Everyone was talking, repeating the word "miracle." No one was interested in Moira's tea, which was just as well because she'd used all the butter which reminded her why she'd come out in the first place. She had to get to the store.

At the corner store, three blocks away, several people were bunched together at the counter, talking. She sidled up behind them. "Jesus' face," they were saying, and "Have you seen it?" Someone was telling somebody else that she wasn't surprised Jesus had shown up because the town was full of sinners. Some of them thought this was true, and others thought it was silly. One person said, "There goes the neighbourhood." Moira thought she didn't need this, and left. She'd get her butter at the supermarket.

It was no better there. People were bunched in the aisles speculating, gesticulating, the word "miracle" on everyone's lips. She heard her name repeated, "Moira Tuttle," and her address. Keeping her face down she walked quickly to the dairy section, found her butter, took it to one of the empty counters and stood there. The clerk disengaged herself from one of the groups to wait on her, took her money, and handed her the butter. "You've come at a bad time," she said cheerfully. "Everybody's talking about some miracle. Nobody wants to work."

Moira, playing dumb, asked "What miracle?"

"There's a face in a tree stump on Montgomery Street. They say it looks just like Jesus. Someone should phone the *National Enquirer* and tell them we've got a scoop. It would knock that JonBenét Ramsey kid off the front page." She looked at the paper with the photo of the dead child model. "This is more uplifting, don't you think? People need something like this instead of all the doom and gloom."

Moira smiled and took her package. Ed, she thought, hurrying out of the store, what have you done?

When she got to her street, she could see from a distance that the crowd had grown. There were several vans parked opposite the stump, and she could make out a TV camera and crew. Clutching her butter, Moira circled the block and entered her house by the back door. She was putting butter in the fridge when the pounding started. "Mrs. Tuttle. Are you there, Mrs. Tuttle?" Oh, Christ, she thought, and immediately regretted it. She would have to let them in. There was nothing else for it. She walked down the hall past the living room, glared briefly at Ed's picture on the mantel, and opened the door.

There were several people from the local paper, a couple of whom she recognized, but a lot she'd never seen before. Flashes went off, momentarily blinding her. She shielded her face. "Mrs. Tuttle, how long has it been there? Did you know it was there when they cut down the tree? Are you religious, Mrs. Tuttle? Do you believe in God?"

"Please," Moira said. "One at a time. I'll answer one question at a time. I didn't know it was there. I'm a Unitarian." There, she thought grimly. Let them sort that one out. If they think that makes me a believer, they'll know more about me than I do.

That, as it turned out, was a mistake. They thought she belonged to a cult. One of them suggested she'd painted the face on the trunk herself, as some kind of ritual. Was she a Wiccan? "It's not paint," she shouted in exasperation. "Get an expert. And it's not Christ's face, it's Ed's."

And who was Ed, they wanted to know, but she'd said the right thing this time. They weren't interested in her Ed. They wanted divine revelation. They left her alone then, and interviewed Lois and Bill. Moira saw them through the window, earnestly expounding, she presumed, on the wonder of it all. They looked sincere which is more, she decided, than I am.

The rest of the week was just as silly. Tree specialists came to determine that, yes, the elm had been a real tree with real bark. Too bad it didn't bite, Moira thought grimly, watching the interview on TV. The curator of the art gallery verified that the image hadn't been painted or etched on, but couldn't say how it got there. There were, apparently, experts coming from Rome. The stump was cordoned off to preserve the image. Various religious leaders appeared in front of it with their flocks in tow. People knelt and wept. Some of them turned away. Moira took to taking her meals in front of the television so as not to miss anything. She was watching the evening news when she heard a knock at the back door.

It was Porter, Ed's best friend. He and Ed had been buddies even before Ed and Moira married. Porter himself had never married. He'd always been part of their lives. Porter pushed his briefcase through the door past Moira, and walked straight to the kitchen where he put it on a chair. "Shhhhh," he said. "They didn't see me come in. That's Ed in the stump."

"Of course it is," Moira replied crossly. "That's who it's always been. Ed doesn't look like Christ. Never did."

"Well," said Porter, "it's no good telling them that. I knew how it would be when I saw how it was, if you get my drift."

"How he got there I can't imagine," Moira said. "Do you have any idea?"

"Beats me," said Ed. "I'm stumped."

Good old Porter. Moira smiled. Salt of the earth and as corny as Kansas in August. She was glad to see him.

Porter took pastrami, sauerkraut, dill pickles, and rye out of his briefcase, and dug to the bottom where he'd buried the beer. Together they fixed smoked meat sandwiches and sat at the table, munching and drinking the cold brew. When they'd finished, they wiped their mouths and looked at each other. Porter lit a cigarette, and Moira put an ashtray in front of him. "Well, Porter," she said smiling. "What do we do now?"

Porter took a long drag. "We'll have to do something. It's going to get worse. The town council's made Thursday disability day. Wheelchairs, crutches, stretchers, they'll all be lined up in front of your house, wanting old Ed to do something. Friday's for everything else. Everything from colds to cancer. And if just one of those people gets cured of anything, the whole planet will be here. If you ever wanted the world at your feet, now's the time to wish for something else. It could happen."

"Do you suppose, Porter," Moira's voice shook a little, "that there's anything to it? Because if there was, I wouldn't want to interfere."

Porter looked at her fondly. "You know Ed couldn't cure hiccups. He's having us all on. He's gonna wait till they're all lined up and gawking at him, and then he'll fade out. Disappear."

"He would," Moira said. "That's just what Ed would do. Fade like the grin on the Cheshire cat."

"And in the meantime," Porter continued, "there's all these people trampling down the lawn and blocking the sidewalk. So here's what we do. Do you have any lye?"

At about one a.m. that morning, Moira and Porter were on their knees in front of the stump. They were wearing rubber gloves. Moira had a bucket and a scrub brush, and Porter carried the lye. Together they put down their equipment and looked at Ed. His smile, Moira thought, seemed a little wider.

"A joke is a joke, Ed," Porter said, "if you get my drift. But we want you to cut it out. This nonsense has gone far enough."

"Ed." Moira was determined. "I don't know where you are or what you think you're doing, but you should stop this. If you don't fade out right now, we'll have to erase you. Rub you out." She looked at Porter and giggled. "I sound like a gangster," she said. "He won't believe me."

"Yeah, he will. Look at him. There he goes."

The face was fading. They watched until it disappeared, all at once, efficiently, till there was nothing left but tree rings on the raw stump. Then they put the lye and scrub brush in the bucket, stripped off their gloves, and went back into the house.

"Well there," said Moira. "It's good he paid attention. Usually I couldn't get him to mind me no matter what I did. I'm glad you came, Porter."

"Well, I figured he wanted me. I know Ed. He always liked attention. Listen, I'd best be off before the neighbours start to talk."

"It's late, Porter," Moira said. And then she heard herself saying, all in a rush, "You might as well spend the night."

Porter smiled. He has a nice quiet smile, thought Moira. It's been a while since I really looked at him.

She smiled back. "You can borrow Ed's pajamas. I'll make you breakfast."

Porter put his briefcase down. "I guess I could stay. If you're sure you don't mind. But what about Ed?"

So that was it, she thought, leading the way upstairs. You devil, Ed. "Oh, no, Porter," she said. "Ed wouldn't mind at all."

Edna Remembers Exactly How It Goes

SHEREE FITCH

In This House Are Many Women and Other Poems, 2004

hey mickey and susie were up in a tree they were
doing the
k-i-s-s-i-n-g-thing
next thing you know
was the wedding bells ringing
and people were singing and ever-y-thing
and waah came the baby
and farmer in the dell
well mickey and susie weren't doing very well
singing ashes ashes
wishes in the well
promises are falling down falling down all
the way to
hell

Little Boy Blue has to pay the bills
Little Miss Muffet's on Valium pills

so mickey said to susie
want to go back to that tree
to the time when we kissed
and the kisses were free

but no king's horses
no king's men
could put those two
back together again

mickey and susie
up in a tree
but when the bough breaks
the cradle falls
down comes everyone
baby and all

The Inertial Observer

CHRIS WEAGLE
Grain, 2002

On one wave's crest, I sit astride
an unobstructed view, and watch
the curved line where the surface turns
to air, and see how we are bound,
tied to the fulcrum of the sun.
There is the cable that swings us
around, like the arm of a boy
who wheels a bucket of water.
The Earth in turn secures the moon,
causing the tide to fret against
the shore as if it wished for more
than a marriage of gravity,
though all it can do is repeat
itself, wearing down, grain by grain.

Aunt Margaret

VICTORIA KRETZSCHMAR EASTMAN
Echoes: The Northern Maine Journal of Rural Culture, 2001

To a little girl Aunt Margaret seemed like a scary picture-book character. Her skin and hair and eyes were colourless. Black cat's-eye glasses tipped with diamonds magnified her enormous, shimmering pupils. Her voice sounded like someone walking on stones. When she smiled, her mouth was stiff and crooked. Her teeth were yellow.

Mama told me that I knew Aunt Margaret before she had her stroke, but I didn't remember. There was a black-and-white picture in my baby book of an elegant white-haired lady with diamond buttons on her black dress. She was helping me cut my first birthday cake. Years later I realized that stylish woman was Aunt Margaret.

When I was three, a stroke changed Aunt Margaret from the lady in the photograph to someone I did not want to be near. She could not use words the way other grown-ups did. Instead, they were short and loud and she had to force them out, like they were trapped behind her teeth. She couldn't move one arm and that hand was like a sharp, white claw.

When we visited Aunt Margaret her smile begged Mama to set me on her lap. Then she would wrap her only moving arm around me and murmur close to my hair. My aunt wanted to see my face. But I thought if I looked into her quaking pupils, they would cast a deathly spell on me. My gaze would move no further than the pearls that followed the black curve of her dress collar.

When Aunt Margaret came to Grandma and Grandpa's for the holidays, I tried very hard to avoid her lap. But grown-ups were always around to pick me up and give me to my aunt. She was so happy to hold me, even though I sat stiff and silent, waiting to be rescued.

My fifth Christmas at my grandparents' house was Aunt Margaret's last with all of us. That year, Papa was taking his traditional Christmas Eve nap and I sat on the floor beside the tree playing with the new doll Mama had given me. Grandpa was in his big black chair writing in a crossword book Grandma had given him. She and Mama were tidying the room so Santa would not trip on anything the next morning. Aunt Margaret was deciding to light another cigarette.

Because her right hand was frozen by the stroke, Aunt Margaret used her left to knock a Kool out of its pack, hold it between her long, white fingers, then place it between her lipstick-red lips. With her right elbow holding the match folder steady, she could strike a match with her left hand and light her smoke by herself. The only thing she could not do was blow out the flame. So she waved the little fire like a tiny blue flag in front of her until only a thin string of smoke remained. Aunt Margaret also had trouble putting out her cigarettes. She even set her bedroom on fire twice.

"Show Aunt Margaret your new doll," Mama said.

Slowly, I picked up my Chatty Cathy, taking time to straighten her dress and smooth her hair. Finally, I took her to my aunt's lap and she stroked Cathy's black curls.

"Pretty." She spit the word out and smiled half a smile.

"She talks, too," I said, pulling the white plastic ring at the back of Chatty's neck.

"I'm sleepy," Chatty said in a singsong voice.

"Oh." Aunt Margaret was impressed.

"I smell smoke," Mama said.

Grandma went to check the stove.

"Can't you smell smoke?" Mama asked Grandpa.

I stood stiffly in front of Aunt Margaret.

"What?" was all my aunt could say.

Then Mama cried out and ran to the bedroom where Papa was sleeping. She was afraid the electric blanket had caught fire. Grandpa followed her, and together they both shouted Papa awake. He hadn't even been using the electric blanket. Then the three of them, Papa with puffy eyes, spread out through the house searching for the smoke Mama smelled. In the pantry Grandma was already pouring water from a glass measuring cup onto hot ashes in the trash can.

"What happened, Grandma?" I asked, after everyone had come back into the living room.

She looked at me, standing in front of Aunt Margaret.

"One of Margaret's cigarettes."

"Oh," I said, climbing onto the couch beside my aunt and sitting Chatty Cathy in my lap. Several times I pulled the string to make her talk, but no one else said anything for a long while.

After that, Aunt Margaret spent Christmases at the private nursing home where she lived. It was an old stone house with two front turrets that reached high above the third floor, into the evening sky. My aunt lived in a huge room on the second floor. The room was brightened by old-fashioned lamps on corner tables and tiny decorated shades hanging from the ceiling patterned in ivory-painted tin. Mama and I visited Aunt Margaret there one Christmas to deliver her present, a pink flannel nightgown and robe with white frills at the collar and sleeves.

"Oh! Oh! Pretty!" Aunt Margaret pointed to the dresser beside her brass bed. On the white runner, embroidered with pink and blue flowers, were several containers shiny like her bed. One was a lipstick holder. Another was a powder dish with a soft beige puff lightly covering the scent. Beside them was a package wrapped in gold paper with a white bow. It was for Mama and me.

"Can I open it, Mama?" I was eight now, and I thought my aunt was a very important person to live in such a beautiful house.

Aunt Margaret nodded and said, "Yes."

It was an electric card shuffler and two brand new decks of cards.

"Neat!" I was impressed. "Like on TV, Mama!"

Mama shook her head at me then said, "Thank you, Margaret."

Trying to fix whatever I had done, I said, "Mama and I play cards all the time."

Aunt Margaret smiled at Mama. "Canasta," she tried to say.

Mama smiled back, "You taught me."

Margaret nodded.

Mama talked to Aunt Margaret long enough for me to make certain our gift really did shuffle cards. Finally satisfied, I returned it to the box and anxiously awaited the opportunity to try out the several decks of cards we had at home.

We wished Aunt Margaret a Merry Christmas as we left her room. Outside, the clear city night sparkled with street lights and Christmas decorations. Mama and I crunched in the snow back to the car where Papa was waiting.

"Did I do something wrong at Aunt Margaret's, Mama?"

"Aunt Margaret buys things she sees on TV because she can't go out shopping," Mama explained. "Mentioning that might make her feel bad."

"It's okay to have things from TV, isn't it?"

"Some people don't like their presents bought from television. It might embarrass Aunt Margaret that she has to buy hers that way."

"Oh," I said, and smiled secretly, glad that Aunt Margaret did, because I knew Mama never would.

Some Christmases we couldn't visit Aunt Margaret. Then, we would mail her a package and she would send us a TV gift and a Christmas card signed in big, crooked letters. The nurses at her home helped guide her hand with the red pen Aunt Margaret liked to use for the holiday.

Eventually, we stopped getting gifts from Aunt Margaret. We knew her Christmas cards were chosen for her by someone who worked at the home. Every year, less and less of Aunt Margaret's name would appear beneath the sentiment of the card. Perhaps new nurses were not as patient to help her print. Maybe Aunt Margaret just wanted to try to write her own name by herself, for a change.

One winter when I was in high school Aunt Margaret died. Because we lived so far away, Mama and Papa decided we could not drive that distance on snowy roads and get to my aunt's funeral in time. Grandma and Grandpa, who lived near Margaret all their lives, had been named executors of my aunt's estate and had stored her belongings in their garage. That summer when we visited my grandparents, Grandma told me to take what I wanted.

I looked through a clothes rack of stylish 1940s and '50s garments. Most of them were in excellent condition, except for a few tiny cigarette burns, which were barely noticeable. Aunt Margaret and I were the same size. I chose a red silk suit with pink glass buttons, a peach jacket with thick shoulder pads, and a black knit dress. It had rhinestone buttons and when I posed in front of the mirror, I realized that this was the dress Aunt Margaret was wearing at my first birthday.

In a small box, I found my aunt's brass lipstick, the red still thick and waxy, and another brass tube the same size with a toothbrush in one end and toothpowder in the other. There was also a small brass pill box and tiny ivory and celluloid spoons to measure medication.

After university, when I finally moved into my first apartment, I kept these trinkets and displayed them on my dresser along with the little book of poetry that was my first birthday gift from Aunt Margaret.

It was *A Child's Garden of Verses* and the brown leather cover had softened to dust. Every poem was printed on a white page that shimmered like satin with borders in gold leaf. Inside the fragile cover, among the pink watercolour roses, was Aunt Margaret's name, as if written with feathers, delicate and graceful, with no hand to guide her.

The Call of the Father

GARY J. LANGGUTH
Malahat Review, 1995

"Qu'est-ce que c'est?"

No answer.

Paul Gagnon turned over in the bed and opened his eyes. Marie was still asleep. The room was chilly and dark.

His hearing was poor, but he could have sworn that he had heard something.

Had he been talking in his sleep? Had Marie? Had he imagined it?

Or... had he heard the call of the father?

"His father called out to him." That was what his Papa, Lucien Gagnon, told him when Grandpère Gagnon died.

"What do you mean, Papa?" he asked. He was only seven at the time.

"I am talking about the call of the father. When a Gagnon gets old, very old, and he is on his deathbed, his father comes to him and calls him home."

Paul squinted several times at the digital clock Yvette had placed on the windowsill. Eleven-thirty. It would be midnight soon, and a New Year. It would also be time to go home. His daughter's house was nice enough, but as far as he was concerned, there was no place like home, and he couldn't wait until he and Marie got back there.

There were nets to be mended, windows to be replaced, seeds to be ordered for spring, a sick friend to be visited in Tracadie. It would be a busy winter. He kissed Marie on the forehead, then lay back on his pillow and shut his eyes.

"Paul."

Paul stared into the darkness. He couldn't believe his ears. It was the clearest thing he had heard in years.

Slaying the Dragon

PATRICK JAMIESON

The Gray Door, 2004

Our clothes are patterns we
Put on to defuse the issue:

Uniforms we adorn to avoid
Change. We wear them not

To change, to sidestep growth.
Look in your wardrobe to see

What you refuse to become.
Before, we used to imagine

We took our clothes off to sin;
Now it is clear, the truth is

Just the opposite. In the sky
The curious cirrus clouds are

A dragon on his back, with his
Feet straight up in the air.

In the chapel, the sun against the
Stained glass, gives an appearance of

Dragon claws, descending: Five talons
Each, on a Chinese Emperor's ornaments.

How we do train our minds to be
Steel boxes aimed at each other:

Bestowing our blessing on this one.
Condemning that one, beyond our control:

Deciding who is holy, intelligent,
Simple, all things fine, worthy of

Our esteem; in comparison, in our
Constriction hardly glimpsing the

Good we leave undone, unimagined.
And, in our attire, we adorn ourselves

In avoiding the issue of our self.

J'aurais crié avec toi

■ HERMÉNÉGILDE CHIASSON
Climats, 1996

c'était l'hiver
le soleil se couchait dans la glace
je te voyais blêmir dans les arbres
leur silhouette noire te goudronner
tu allumais la lampe
la maison sentait l'huile
je rentrais du froid
j'apprenais la noirceur
ton regard d'Indien aux yeux bleus
la flamme dans la maison secouée par le vent
les étincelles dans la nuit
ton cœur craquait de mystère
j'étais ton enfant au sens large du mot
j'étais aussi l'enfant du feu et du froid
je m'endormais dans ta voix
je ne doutais de rien
tu aurais dû me dire de ne jamais étudier le doute
tu aurais dû mettre ton panache
tu aurais dû sortir dans la nuit et crier
et je serais sorti avec toi
et nous aurions fait taire le vent
et toutes les malédictions qu'il répandait sur nous
mais tu ne voulais pas que la nouvelle s'ébruite

I Would Have Cried Out with You

Translation by JO-ANNE ELDER and FRED COGSWELL

Climates, 1999

it was winter
the sun was setting in the ice
I saw you turn pale between the trees
tar-covered by their black silhouette
you lit the lamp
the house smelled of oil
I came in out of the cold
I was learning about the darkness
your blue-eyed Indian gaze
the flame in a wind-shaken house
sparks in the night
your heart crackled with mystery
I was your child in the broad sense of the word
I was also the child of fire and cold
I fell asleep in your voice
I had no doubts
you should have told me never to study doubt
you should have put on your panache
you should have walked into the night and cried out
and I would have gone out with you
and we could have silenced the wind
and all the curses it was spreading over us
but you didn't want the news to spread

et te servais de ta voix pour m'endormir
j'ai appris la noirceur et le silence
j'ai appris la peur d'être emporté par le vent
je sais comme toi ce qu'il faut dire
aux enfants qui ont de la misère a s'endormir
est-ce là la cause de notre si grand sommeil
je sais tout ça pour toujours
il est trop tard pour désapprendre
je sais que d'autres enfants naîtront
ils s'enchaîneront comme des travailleurs
ils diront trop tard qu'on peut faire mentir le vent
dire que le vent peut souffler pour nous
il suffit de croire au pouvoir des mots
il suffit de brandir son cri
ne jamais s'excuser du froid
ne jamais s'excuser de la noirceur
ne jamais s'excuser de rien
faire comme si ce rien contenait notre secret
et vivre avec comme une blessure enfin dissimulée
une blessure qui s'est enfin fermée.

you used your voice to put me to sleep
I learned darkness and silence
I learned to fear being swept away by the wind
I know as well as you do what you have to say
to children who have trouble getting to sleep
is this the reason for our deep sleep
I know all this forever
it is too late to unlearn it
I know other children will be born
they will string themselves out like an assembly line
they will say too late that you can make the wind lie
say that the wind can blow for us
all it takes is belief in the power of words
all it takes is to brandish your cry
never apologize for the cold
never apologize for the dark
never apologize for anything
act as though this nothingness can keep our secret
and live with it like a wound finally hidden
a wound that has healed at last

Little Napoleon

KATHY MAC

Grain, 2007

Napolena? A spoiled grump and toady, ears sleek
as Josie Pye's ringlets, with a knack for ingratiation
where it mattered, bullying where it didn't. Amanda
veered clear of this sister, brawn routed by cunning.

At dinner, the muzzle of the monarch nudged elbows
into surrendering her due, a spoonful of soufflé, perhaps
a tidbit of fish, carefully de-boned, especially after
her embolism—airlifted to PEI for two weeks

of doggy-wheelchair racing in the animal hospital's halls.
She returned Richard-the-Third lame, requiring
twice-daily physio, chauffeuring to twice-weekly
acupuncture at the naturopathic veterinary in Truro.

Through it all, she charmed, except when charm failed.
Then she growled, a four-cylinder tractor. The runt ruled.

From Combat to Cocktails on Clock Street

JILL VALÉRY

Globe and Mail, May 13, 2004

It's very cold today in San Miguel. Marta stands on the step of her shoe store, waiting.

Diminutive and elegant, her grey wool coat matches her grey wool dress, though she is not wearing the signature wide-brimmed hat I've observed on two previous visits. Her black hair is layered, very short, her eyelashes very long and thick. Her expression is both peaceful and alert. She is strikingly beautiful. At some signal from Marta, who has turned sideways, an employee stands behind her and places her arms around Marta's tiny waist, gently lifting her from the step to the sidewalk. I'm riveted by this tender gesture, far too delicate, too intimate for this busy street with its inquisitive eyes. Marta takes a few deliberate, awkward steps. A taxi pulls up. The employee runs after her, reaches forward to help. As I turn away, I notice Marta's flat-heeled, black leather shoes, unwieldy flatirons clamped to each fragile foot.

In the last four years, I have acquired nine pairs of the shoes Marta's husband designs. "San Miguel Shoe: Cocktail, Combat Sandals and more" reads the small notice tucked inside each purchase. My first two pairs had tire-tread soles for doing combat with the steep, sharp-stoned streets of another Mexican town. Subsequent pairs had lower heels but were just as blissfully comfortable. This year, I bought cocktail shoes with a two-inch heel and a toe-thong. All nine pairs are made with leather-braced wide-banded elastic. They look elegant and feel like gloves for the feet. The non-slip soles are essential for San Miguel's uneven cobbled streets and narrow sidewalks worn by centuries of footsteps to the sheen and danger of black ice.

Inside the *Tienda Marta*, hundreds of white shoeboxes are piled high against every wall of the narrow two-storey building, all but obscuring the entrance window displays. Shoes and boxes frequently cascade to the floor as employees search for different sizes, sometimes scaling a small ladder set against this precarious cardboard wall. Customers can barely move inside the store, but business is brisk, and most will leave with two or three pairs of these irresistible shoes. Even if I buy nothing, I visit the store every two or three days for the pure aesthetic pleasure of standing in the midst of myriad textures and styles and a riot of colours: peacock-blue, scarlet, fuchsia, silver and bronze, purple, yellow and lime.

As a young girl, I grew up in a family of very limited means. My mother made most of our clothes, often from unorthodox sources. A blanket became a winter jacket, a linen tablecloth a sundress, and a sheet dyed yellow was transformed into my school's requisite summer uniform. When I went to university, my mother made me a beautiful lined coat in olive green wool and a slim Prince of Wales check skirt with a kick pleat in the back. There was nothing she was unable to knit or sew for us. Except shoes.

My hunger for beautiful footwear has its roots in those years of shoe famine. Clumsy school lace-ups and various hand-me-downs were eked out like crumbs while I longed with all my heart for a pair of strappy sandals. One day, I decided to make a pair. I bought two sets of cork insoles and some bias binding which I knotted through holes poked at intervals along the edge of each sole after gluing right and left tops and bottoms together. I slipped them on, criss-crossing the flimsy binding around my ankles: my very own Roman sandals, made to measure! I felt not only happy but full, as though I'd just eaten a sumptuous meal. And I still felt full even when my creation disintegrated in the first downpour of the afternoon. Later, when I was able to buy shoes more or less when I wanted, I continued to see shoes as food. Why else would my heart leap at the mention of buttery leather boots in shades of chestnut and coffee, creamy suede shoes in caramel and chocolate, or sandals in luscious, summery confections of lime, orange, and strawberry?

As I venture once more down Clock Street to Marta's store, I ponder the paradox of the cacti which feature so prominently in the photo advertising San Miguel Shoe. In spite of its spiny, rebarbative appearance, the cactus is also a food. *Nopales,* the de-thorned leaves of the plant, are a subtle delicacy in many a Mexican dish. In this photo, one sandal hangs by its heel from a spiky green column; others are placed on an equal footing, as it were, with more sharp-leaved cacti. The image seems to offer a clue to the relationship between Marta and the shoes that surround her every day, shoes that she will never be able to wear. I imagine that if my feet were distorted with arthritis, those once-addictive shoes would be yet another source of pain, thorns for the feet instead of gloves. But there is consolation in the thought that if I could not dance in those shoes, then those shoes might still dance within me, in their vibrant colours and perfect symmetry. Only Marta could say with certainty.

The Prince of Fortara and The Flat Earth

RAYMOND FRASER

When The Earth Was Flat, 2007

One day while I was visiting Windsor Castle the Prince of Fortara brought a curious incident to my attention. He had been leafing through a genealogy newsletter and happened upon a letter from Lord Louis Mountbatten concerning an article I had published in *Weekend Magazine*. The article, as I recall, was entitled "Royally Wronged," and dealt with the case of one James Stewart of Blacks Harbour, New Brunswick, who claimed to be the rightful heir to the throne of England, Ireland, Scotland, and France.

Lord Mountbatten mentioned showing my story to Queen Elizabeth II, and remarked that "the Queen was amused." Whether she said, "We are amused," can only be surmised, but I would hope she did. Since her ancestor Queen Victoria is best remembered for her statement, "We are not amused," the present queen might find a similarly memorable place in history for her own pithy comment.

Most people reading the above would not have a clue what I'm talking about, but it's a true story.

A man's home is his castle, and there are Windsor Castles and Windsor Castles. One is in England, which readers of the British tabloids are quite familiar with. Another is situated on Windsor Street, in Fredericton, and was for some years the residence of the Prince of Fortara, otherwise known as Alden Nowlan.

⁘

Alden wasn't born a prince, any more than I was born the Duke of Northumberland. We both came from humble beginnings and had to go out into the world and acquire our titles.

Although my friendship with Alden covered twenty-two years, from 1961 to his death in 1983, what I know of his childhood I've learned mostly from his writings, and from dipping into some later (and not always reliable) biographies. Alden talked a good deal about his father, a rough hard-drinking man, but never once mentioned his mother, who abandoned him and his sister when they were quite young. It wasn't until many years after we met that I learned he had a sister. I still to this day couldn't tell you exactly where in Nova Scotia he came from. He called the place Desolation Creek—later Ketapasa Creek—and would say it in all seriousness, and that was as much as you could get out of him, drunk or sober.

⁘

I began corresponding with Alden in 1961, but didn't meet him until a year later when another young writer, LeRoy Johnson, and I visited him in Hartland. I was sober on that occasion, and again on my last visits to Windsor Street in 1982 and 1983; but never during the intervening years. For all the nights I spent at his place I can't for the life of me remember what bed or couch I slept on. Claudine was always there, of course, brimming with life and good humour; and son Johnny at times, when he wasn't off to sea as a merchant mariner.

I'm not really sure what I can say about Alden in a few words (which is what I've allowed myself, so I won't put this off forever). His work speaks for itself and has only to be read to be appreciated. When I first wrote him back in 1961—having seen his poetry in Fred Cogswell's *Fiddlehead* magazine—I was twenty and living in my home town of Chatham. By this time I was several years into my own writing and drinking careers. Alden replied and our correspondence eventually ran to 160 or so letters each.

We got together on a good many occasions over the years. As a veteran boozer from the Miramichi once observed, a man's got ten good years of drinking in him, and from then on it's all downhill. I'd say my ten good ones coincided with Alden's, from roughly the mid-sixties to the mid-seventies.

We had wonderfully lively parties in those days at Windsor Castle. Like one of his heroes, Samuel Johnson, Alden with a libation in hand was a brilliant conversationalist and story teller. It was unfortunate for the public he never found fame enough in his lifetime to become a feature personality on things like TV talk shows. It was also unfortunate he didn't have a sober Boswell around to record his monologues. The drinking nights were fun, but they had a way of dimming if not entirely erasing the memory.

It wasn't all one-sided at his house. There was frequently a spirited crowd around him, people who could keep the show going, a lot of give and take and flights of fancy. Alden's inseparable friend, the philosopher Leo Ferrari, was probably his most frequent guest, but visitors were always coming through the door, young poets and writers like Al Pittman, Louis Cormier, Bernell MacDonald, Jim Stewart, Eddie Clinton, Lindsay Buck, David Richards, Terry Crawford, and Dave Butler. Also some older, long-time friends like Fred Cogswell and Bob Gibbs. And an assortment of army officers, politicians, newspaper editors, painters, musicians, and what have you.

It was on one of these gatherings, in 1970, that the Flat Earth Society was formed. There were four of us in the living room that night, Alden, Leo, Sharon — my good wife of those days — and myself. I remember Alden and I playing with the concept of planoterrestrialism, and discovering (as might have been expected from two such radically progressive thinkers) that we were both sympathetic to the idea.

The philosophy of planoterrestrialism is too deep and extensive to go into here, so I'll merely say that after finding ourselves in accord, Alden turned to Leo Ferrari and said, "Leo, do you believe the earth is flat?" And without a second thought, Leo — who was discussing something with Sharon — turned and said, "Of course it's flat. Any fool can see that!"

Apparently it was an idea whose time had come, because before too many months had passed we were issuing tracts, had an irregular newsletter, and could boast a worldwide membership of close to two hundred. Alden wrote a story about the society for *Weekend Magazine*, and Leo—by now the FES President—became a much sought-after speaker on the banquet circuit. My position was Chairman of the Board of Directors, while Alden—having his choice in the matter—adopted the title of Symposiarch.

▪▪

As fast as we were ascending in the world, we were to go even higher, when Alden discovered that the young poet, Jim Stewart, was most surely a descendant of the House of Stewart, the criminally deposed and rightful rulers of England, Ireland, Scotland, and France.

We gathered a few hundred adherents there as well. With King James in a position to reward the faithful, the world quickly acquired a new aristocracy, with titles flying about left, right, and centre. Alden became Prince of Fortara, Leo the Archbishop of Canterbury, and myself the Duke of Northumberland and First Lord of the Admiralty. Everyone we knew and many we didn't were transformed overnight into Lords and Ladies of the realm.

And, as mentioned, when the usurper, Queen Elizabeth II, read my story about our movement, she affected to be amused. Not a word about her head's uneasy nights on the pillow.

There were bright times like the day Alden and Claudine and King James and Queen Jane came over to the Miramichi to inspect the Royal Navy. Before setting out to sea Alden christened the navy—my converted lobster boat, *Spanish Jack*—with a pint of Schooner beer, the champagne of the new nobility. It was no great decision deciding against the destruction of a good quart of wine.

■■

As everyone knows, a great many writers have been drinkers. Someone mentioned the other night that of the seven Americans who've won the Nobel Prize, six were alcoholics. The condition is not a disgrace, it's an affliction. In 1982 I reached the end of my own particular rope and began going to meetings, which got me off the stuff and so far has kept me that way.

Alden mentioned the subject in a number of his letters to me, and it was something we talked about from time to time. If nothing else, in his case, he had diabetes, and it's not a good idea for a diabetic to touch alcohol. He was aware of the problem but averse to the solution. He couldn't imagine himself giving up the bottle entirely, he said, pointing out that if it weren't for alcohol he'd never have had the nerve to ask Claudine out, and so wouldn't be married to her now. As if he owed some kind of loyalty to the stuff.

The worst effect my drinking had on me was the loneliness I came to experience. People seem to disappear from your life, and if there are any still around they often don't want to have much to do with you—for good reasons—and you begin to think there is no one else like you in all the world. You can be in the midst of a hundred people and know that feeling. It's like an emptiness of the spirit, a lost and desperate feeling, a sense of total abandonment. It's what leads a great many drinkers to suicide, if something else doesn't get them first.

After I got sober Alden called me up a few times. Once he said he was out of gin and asked me to get him a bottle. I did, and found him in quite wretched shape when I got there, a condition I'd seen myself in often enough. He wasn't out of gin; he had half a dozen bottles in the cupboard; he just needed company. Another time it was for cigarettes, which he already had.

In one way and another, what I've mentioned can be found in his poetry, fiction, essays, and letters. When I first wrote him, back in 1961, it was a fan letter. I was always in search of heroes, and saw one in him; then inevitably he proved a fellow mortal, and became something of real value, a friend.

He revealed a lot about himself in his writings, more than in person, and it's what I like most about his work. We get to know him there, and feel a kinship, see ourselves. It's the highest purpose of writing, in my opinion, linking one human spirit with another.

I was in Paris when Sharon wrote and told me Alden had died. I was still some years away from being able to cry but I got a tightness in the chest and a lump in the throat. I took a walk along the Seine thinking about him. I knew what I missed already, and it was to come to me different times after that. Alden was one of the rare people who understood. When something strikes you, and you think, Alden will know what I mean, and you look forward to telling him, knowing you're not going to get a blank look.... And then you realize, well, I can't do that now. It's like losing a part of yourself.

The Gift of Life at the Wandlyn

STEWART DONOVAN
Descant, 1998

Winter donors crowd the corridor in this roadside
        motel. We take tickets, but it's as casual
as *Canadian Tire*. Line-ups. Queues they call them
        in Dublin, London. They're UN-AMERICAN,
of course. Leftenant, Lewtenant. Liqueur, Liqor.
        Identity hangs on a phoneme.
Hang up (*for Christ's sake)* it's long distance
        from the Maritimes.
Some of these donors look like refugees (or is it
        me?) awaiting the paper of hope, the stamp of
despair. A mother nursing her newborn ignores the
        impatient émigré in the beard and voice of an
ancient Amish. Unheeded he announces his origin
        as Saint John Loyalist, but looks like he might
protest transfusion instead of insisting to be next.
        We begin to circulate and the HARVEY'S sign across
the street pulses neon (red?), amid the soft wet snow of
        March it revives a school-day memory
crammed full and forgotten: William Harvey,
        English physician, anatomist. 1628, circulation
of the blood. Heart as pump, mechanistic mind,
        De Motu Cordis et Sanguinis, motions of the heart

and blood. Motions indeed: *We can't go on like this.*
No one does now. No one, not even for the kids.
Motions of the heart and mind. Mechanistic thinking.
The body and blood.
No one else is rushed, seems anxious to stretch
themselves upon the gurney for penetration:
least of all myself. I've never needed blood and secretly
and shamefully begrudge the giving. What am I
doing here? Is it pride at being able to hide the childish
fear in stoic smiles that brings me round again?
or memory of my mother leaving home by the back
door on a stretcher the young Mountie couldn't
carry? Boyish face contorted in sweating strain over
the outport hill too steep for Cadillac undercarriage.
Huddled in hot fear, hemorrhage was the word we heard
Aunt Helen nods across kitchen tiles to a younger
sister still unconscious of racial memories—Celtic
Catholic grandmothers, blood and bone buried again
and again under forty. Miscarriage. Motions of the heart
and mind. Mechanistic thinking.

Clutching number thirty-three (what else!) I'm next.
The nurse disarms me (they always do), told to hold
out my arms for inspection I imagine myself in some
Hollywood film noir, recovering poet: desperate
Coleridge seeking another Kubla Khan, or Mr.
Holmes relieving boredom until the next nurse
takes my wrist and pin pricks my index back to the
business at hand. The forms we file remind me of
my gay friend whose blood they will not take unless he
lies about how he sleeps and loves, changes the
motions of his heart and mind. Mechanistic thinking.
Miscarriage.

Blood runs fast this warm March afternoon so I head for
the recovery cot in record time. Staffed today by
professional hockey wives: glamourous volunteers they
move like hummingbirds beside the beehive
women in white. Blonde hair, bracelets and a showgirl
smile hides an Iowa farm woman who likes us but
longs for her folks and the wide fields of home. She asks
if I go to the games and I confess no, not since my
boys stopped collecting cards. I don't mention my last
time in the arena, but recall early September
wandering with my Belgian friend among the patches of
the Canadian quilt that covered the concrete floor
awaiting the ice of October.

Leaving the rink my friend says I must visit Ypres
(Epres? Eeper! he insists, he's Flemish not Walloon!)
He smiles then, and says the dead obey no language laws.
No doubt the Red Cross carried the gassed
Canadian boys (soldiers are always boys) from the sea of
green and watched their last moments in pure air
under canvas tents. It was always a business of
course, we simply never saw it so. Those images of
war and relief of famine and flood tainted now and swept
forever under waves of grief, cries of innocence.
De Motu Cordis et Sanguinis

Harry Forestell: A Man Ahead of Our Time

MARK GIBERSON

Carleton University Magazine, 2006

Harry Forestell is right where he wants to be—five time zones ahead of most of the competition. Since this past November, Forestell has been telling sleepy-eyed Canadians what's been going on in the world while they've been snug in their beds.

As co-host of CBC television's *CBC News: Morning*, Forestell begins his workday around six a.m. But unlike his viewers—and his competition in other networks—Forestell, forty-four, lives and works in London, England. And that makes Forestell literally one-of-a-kind—the only host of a North American television morning show who's stationed outside the continent.

"I'm awake and ready to roll hours before Canada wakes up," says Forestell. "When our viewers start tuning in to the show around six o'clock in the morning, I'm there to give them the rundown on what's been happening around the world for the last six to twelve hours. I'm there to help them understand the breaking news, too—what's happening right now. And I think what's important is that I'm here on the ground, outside of Canada, helping our viewers see the world through Canadian eyes."

Before "international editor" was added to his title last August, Forestell was co-anchoring the morning news show from Toronto. "Mornings have always been my beat, from the time I worked with CBC Radio in Ottawa," says Forestell. "There's something about getting up early and getting ahead of everybody else, knowing what the day holds. I've always enjoyed that."

According to Forestell, CBC's decision to move him and his family to London was a direct response to a network study of viewer preferences. "We found that Canadians want more foreign coverage," he says. "In part, this is due to changing demographics. A lot of new Canadians have family members overseas. They want to stay in touch with the world beyond our borders. But most Canadian broadcasters have been cutting back on their overseas bureaus. CBC decided to listen to its viewers and buck the trend."

Forestell's new post was confirmed by the network last July. Days later, terrorist bombings rocked the British capital, leaving death and destruction in their wake. Forestell recalls the conversation he had with his wife, Jenny, the night after the terrorist attacks. "I remember asking Jenny, 'How do you feel now about going over there with our two girls?' Her response was, 'If I could be there sooner, I would. We can't let these people determine our future. I'm more determined than ever to go.'"

Forestell explains that his British wife had lived in London through the '80s and early '90s when IRA bombings were a common occurrence. "Jenny is pretty emblematic of the attitude you find among most Londoners," he says. "Memories of the blitz are still close to the surface. This city has been through harder times and survived." So, the couple—and their daughters, Patricia, four, and Erin, two—took off for London, where they had lived, and where Forestell had worked as a freelancer, five years earlier. They arrived just one week before a fifty-day lockout severed the ties between CBC viewers and the corporation's on-air personalities, Forestell included.

"We finally went to air on November 7," says Forestell. "It was a brilliant, blue-sky day—a rarity for London—and we were broadcasting live from Trafalgar Square. I was surprised by the number of Canadians who came up to us as we were shooting. People from the Maritimes, folks from Alberta, others from Ontario—all eager to see the morning show back on the air."

In the weeks that followed, Forestell was interviewing author Salman Rushdie and Canadian rock star and photographer Bryan Adams. “It’s an amazing feeling to be back in London,” says Forestell. “And it’s even more amazing to be over here with a news crew and a satellite truck. We’re Canada’s eyes and ears, on location. It doesn’t get much better than this.”

Ode on a North American Desk

CHRIS WEAGLE
Fiddlehead, 2000

You, unvarnished table with sun faded
pigments like fired clay bereft of glaze,
become a sylvan metaphor of desk.
Looped grains swirl in rivers and ruminate
on design as careful etchings bloom in
figure-eights like lovers ever entwined.
Your tabular print is hidden within
Aristotelian oak, whose seed once strived
to potential, grew to be hewn and shaved,
grew to bear these beveled buttresses
and conical legs. Stripped of varnish, you rest
in this basement beside sandpaper creased
like cramped knuckles. When you gleam again
it will be like glossy vinyl hinting
at old melodies within its grooves.
When old age takes this generation
your drawers will hold their photographs.

St. Leonard's Revisited

AL PITTMAN

An Island in the Sky: Selected Poetry of Al Pittman, 2003

We came ashore
where wildflower hills
tilted to the tide
and walked
sad and gay
among the turnip cellars
tripping over the cremated
foundations
of long-ago homes
half buried
in the long years' grass

Almost reverently
we walked among the rocks
of the holy church
and worshipped roses
in the dead yard
and came again to the cove
as they did after rosary
in the green and salty days

And men offshore
hauling traps

wondered what ghosts
we were
walking with the forgotten sheep
over the thigh-high grass paths
that led
like trap doors
to a past
they could hardly recall

Historic Fredericton

WILLIAM A. SPRAY

Impressions of Historic Fredericton, 1998

This book is an attempt to show the beauty and variety of the buildings which make Fredericton and the surrounding area such an attractive place. Fernando Poyatos has always felt there was something special about many of these buildings, and several years ago he began to paint those which he found artistically interesting and challenging. He also began to ask questions about the buildings. Who constructed them and when? Who lived in them, or what were they used for? In 1994 he asked me to collaborate with him on a book that would include some of his paintings and some information about the buildings.

Finding buildings of historic interest in the Fredericton area was not a very difficult task, but deciding which ones to include in the book was more complicated. The final choice came down to those which had some historical interest or uniqueness and those which best reflected the artist's style and feeling for Fredericton. Many buildings of perhaps equal or greater interest were excluded, but it was impossible to include them all.

The major feature of Fredericton is the beautiful St. John River and its broad, level plain, which provided a perfect site for a settlement. The earliest settlers of the area were the Native people, the Wolustukwiyik, and their settlement and graveyard were located at St. Anne's Point, near where Government House now stands. In later years the French under Governor Villebon constructed a fort at the mouth of the Nashwaak, and by the 1730s, Acadian settlers had established themselves at St. Anne's Point. In 1759, this settlement was destroyed by the English, leaving few European settlers in the area.

The first Loyalists arrived in 1783 and the construction of houses began almost immediately. The town plat was laid out in 1784, the year the province was created, and St. Anne's Point, now Fredericton, became the provincial capital. Many government buildings were constructed, among them the oldest public building in Fredericton, which stands next to the present Legislature. The city also became the centre for military operations in the province, and some of the old buildings used by the soldiers can still be seen in the Military Compound.

The centre of business activity in the early years was the downriver end of Queen Street and Waterloo Row, where there were a number of inns, a trading post, and stores. As the centre of government developed on Queen Street, so did a new active business district, and the downriver area below the government buildings became a residential area for politicians, government officials, and prominent businessmen. Farraline Place, once a store and trading post, and the former McLeod's Inn, near the corner of Waterloo Row and University Avenue, are two of the few buildings in this area that have survived from the earlier years.

The first church in Fredericton was a chapel constructed by the Jesuits at St. Anne's Point in the first half of the eighteenth century. By the end of the century, the Loyalists had constructed the first Anglican church near the site of the present Christ Church Cathedral. Other religious denominations followed, and their steeples soon dominated the town plat. Fredericton became the site of the first Church of England cathedral built since the Protestant Reformation, and because of this it was often referred to as "the celestial city." It also became the site of King's College, the oldest university building in Canada still in use.

Architecturally and artistically, Fredericton buildings have a fascination for many people and reflect many styles and traditions, from the plain to the very elaborate and ostentatious. Stuart Smith, a former University of New Brunswick art historian, says in *Heritage Handbook* that the Loyalists introduced Georgian architecture to New Brunswick and the idea of style to building construction. A major change in architectural style took place after the construction of Christ Church Cathedral. In his highly informative book *On Earth as It Is in Heaven: Gothic Revival Churches of Victorian New Brunswick,* Gregg Finley says that Christ Church Cathedral "more than any other single building...symbolized the arrival of the Gothic revival in New Brunswick." Gothic Revival was followed by the construction of buildings in imitation of Neo-Grecian, Roman, Italian Renaissance, and other architectural styles.

What interests me most is the history of the buildings and the people who lived and worked in them. I find it almost impossible to walk around Fredericton and not be reminded of some part of its history. A visit to St. Anne's Point and Government House evokes images of Wolustukwiyik canoes arriving there in 1763 to inform New England surveyors attempting to lay out a township grant that the land belonged to them. One can imagine an 1840s party at Government House, with its verandas and gardens stretching down to the river, the ladies and gentlemen arriving in fancy gowns, top hats, or full dress military uniforms, while cooks and servants sweated in the kitchens preparing food. One can also imagine "Boss" Gibson's train pulling out of Marysville and crossing the old railway bridge loaded with mill workers and their families heading off for a picnic.

The face of Fredericton is constantly changing. Walking along King and Queen streets you can admire the few old buildings still standing and study the renovations that keep old structures such as the railway bridge serviceable. It is good to have reminders of what life once was like. Who knows? Perhaps fifty years from now people will stare at what was once a neighbourhood convenience store on some Fredericton corner. They may wonder what it was like to shop in such a place.

Prairie Landscape

TONY STEELE

Impossible Landscapes, 2005

his version

we stand inside an immense circle—
that clump of trees is not the true rim
of the world only some bush gone wild
that protects a farm now sinking in the soil

this imagined circle has no true centre though
the weather-worn boards of the ruined farm
imply a centre—we want to map the world
around hearths even where they are not

the broken, crooked radii on which we walk
stagger outwards from one nothing to another
we desert no truly human homestead
as we voyage outward dream-driven and empty

her version

children played here once—I hear their bones
twist under the wormy sod—the air is dry.
Just now and over there are two streams
that meander underground to that river
beyond the hill almost at the edge of sight
all around us—I breathe the secret springs

bubbling up almost to the prairie grass
oozing between the legs of the fallen ones
sowed on these plains before the plows—
they gave birth in these invisible waters
moaned ecstatic cries and set loose the children
who now play hide-and-seek beneath my feet

El Jardín de las Glicinas

NELA RIO

The Space of Light/El Espacio de la luz, 2005

El rumor llegaba en el perfume. Las flores se tocaban, se inclinaban unas sobre otras, rozaban tallos, se sacudían tentativas y frágiles. El aroma, en racimos penetrantes y azules, se hacía parte de la brisa en esa tarde de primavera. El tronco delgado y las ramas como dedos largos pegados contra la pared, retorcidos, como sufrientes, eran de un marrón oscuro, a veces veteado con blanco grisáceo. Las flores de la glicina parecían pertenecer a otro cuerpo, eran tan brillantes y frágiles y fragantes. La planta no tenía hojas en primavera, sólo el cuerpo que siempre parecía viejo y las flores y el perfume. La glicina estaba contra una pared de ladrillo. El contraste del azul contra el rojo apagado era sorprendente. Hasta se podían ignorar el tronco y las ramas para que sólo quedaran el azul contra el rojo, y el perfume. También había otras flores y era curioso que, aunque cambiaran, la glicina permanecía contra la pared de ladrillo, siempre en flor.

El cuarto estaba a oscuras. La puerta cerrada, sin llave. Ella agachada y abrazándose las rodillas, estaba en el suelo, tratando de desaparecer detrás de la cama. El bebé lloraba en el otro cuarto. Ella empujó unos papeles debajo de la cama. Él entró, no le costó encontrarla. Fue hacia ella y la abrazó "Mi niña, mi amor..." la hizo poner de pie y sentarse en la cama. "Mira esas lágrimas, no, no llores" y le besaba la cara "mi niña, mi amor." La rodeó con los brazos y la acunó, chasqueando la lengua, apaciguándola. La separó unos pocos centímetros de sí mismo, "Mira, mira cómo tienes la

The Wisteria Garden

Translation by ELIZABETH GAMBLE MILLER
The Space of Light/El Espacio de la luz, 2005

The soft murmur was coming from the perfume. The flowers were touching, bending over one another, their stems lightly brushing and quivering, tentative and frail. The aroma, from the intense, blue clusters, permeated the breeze of that spring afternoon. The vine's slim trunk and its long fingers, twisted as if in pain, clinging to the wall, were a dark maroon colour with occasional greyish white streaks. The wisteria flowers, glistening, delicate, and so fragrant, seemed to belong to another body. In springtime the plant had no leaves, only the vine, that always looked old, with its flowers and their perfume. On the brick wall they made a striking contrast of vivid blue against faded red. So striking you might not even see the trunk and branches and notice only the blue against the red, and the perfume. Other flowers sometimes blossomed; curiously, although they might change, the wisteria against the brick wall was always in bloom.

The room was dark. The door was closed, but not locked. Huddled on the floor behind the bed, clutching her knees, she was trying to disappear. She pushed some papers under the bed. In the other room the baby was crying. He came in and easily found her, "Honey, sweetheart..." He forced her to get up and sat her down on the bed, "Now look at those tears, no, no, don't cry," and he kissed her cheek, "Honey, baby." He put his arms around her cuddling her, clicking his tongue, calming her down. Then he moved her slightly

cara... mi amor... no me lo hagas hacer más... si no insistieras con tus cosas yo no lo haría... mira, mira, tu carita..." y ahora era él quien lloraba, gimiendo, pidiendo perdón... "No me lo hagas hacer más, por favor por favor... rompamos ahora esas pinturas... así, así... ya ves, si pintaras flores sería distinto... pero insistes..." Él no vio una de las pinturas que había quedado debajo de la cama. La llevó al baño y quiso lavarle la cara. El bebé había dejado de llorar. Ella también. Él ya no gemía. Ahora era ella la que quería lavarle los nudillos de la mano derecha, ligeramente ensangrentados, "es todo mi culpa... perdóname... pintaré sólo flores"... "¿Me lo prometes? preguntó con cara y gesto de mimoso... "Sí, mi amor."

Siguieron días felices, otros no tanto. Los pedidos de perdón y la insistencia de no hacerlo nunca más crecieron tanto como el niño. Con el tiempo ella se hizo famosa en su pequeña ciudad por sus coloridas pinturas, siempre con flores muy vistosas.

Se encontraba con Pepita, una de sus mejores amigas, todos los martes por la tarde a tomar un té con "tonterías," como le llamaban a todo lo que comían gustosas. Bueno, quizás no todos los martes. Había algunos en que llamaba a Pepita por teléfono y cancelaba la cita. Las razones fueron, al principio, muy complicadas, con caídas de escaleras o tropezones a la entrada del edificio, o que un muchachito la había embestido con la bicicleta, etc. etc. Con los años, Isolina, había perdido el interés por inventar historias y sólo bastaba decir "hoy no puedo" para que Pepita entendiera. Quizás se hizo más difícil cuando su hijo llegó a la adolescencia y aprendió el juego de las recompensas a través de la amenaza y el temor. Isolina, que pintaba algunas veces en un cuarto a oscuras y otras en otro muy iluminado, se iba haciendo chiquita y no hacía ruido en la casa que ya, o quizás nunca, le había pertenecido. Una vez Pepita le comenzó a decir "tendrías que terminar con esto de... no deberías tolerar..." Isolina había abierto los ojos muy grandes y le había puesto punto final con la mirada. Pepita no insistió nunca más. Sabiendo de donde venían, Isolina encontraba folletos dentro de libros o revistas, en la canasta de las frutas, con información sobre conductas muy horribles que nada tenían que ver con ella o con su familia. Rompía los folletos, mientras miraba para otra parte.

away, "Look, oh look at your face...sweetheart...don't make me do it any more...if you just weren't so stubborn about your stuff, I wouldn't do it...look, look at your little face..." Now he was the one crying, moaning, pleading to be forgiven... "Don't make me do it any more, please...please...let's tear up those paintings...here, like this...you see, if you would just paint flowers it would be different...but you insist..."

He didn't see one of the paintings still under the bed. He took her to the bathroom and attempted to wash her face. The baby stopped crying. So did she. And he stopped moaning. Now she was the one wanting to wash the bit of blood off the knuckles of his right hand, "It's all my fault...please forgive me...I'll just paint flowers..." "You promise?" he whimpered in his pampered way... "Yes, honey."

Then came happy days, but others not so. Scenes—pleading to be forgiven, promising not to do it again—grew as rapidly as did their son. As time passed, she became famous in the town for her colourful paintings, always of bright, showy flowers.

Every Tuesday she and her best friend, Pepita, would have "tea and nonsense," the nonsense being everything they ate with relish. Well, not every Tuesday. Sometimes she cancelled out. At first, giving complicated reasons, she fell on the steps, slipped on the sidewalk, a kid on a bicycle ran into her, and so on. But years passed and Isolina lost interest in inventing stories, and "I can't today" was enough for Pepita to understand.

Maybe it was harder when her son became a teenager and learned to trade threats and fear for what he wanted. Whether she was painting in an unlit room or in a bright light, Isolina was becoming so small she scarcely made any noise when she moved about in that house which now, or perhaps, never had belonged to her. Once Pepita blurted out "You've got to stop...you shouldn't stand..."; Isolina's eyes flew wide open; her look added the final period. Pepita never mentioned it again. But Isolina would find pamphlets in a book or magazine or a fruit basket, horrible stories that had nothing to do with her or her family, and she could guess where they came from. She looked away as she tore them up.

Cada vez que vendía uno de los cuadros volvía a la casa con cierta tristeza que nadie se explicaba. Como el día en que en la galería de arte le dieron una mención de honor por "Begonias" y ella casi no sonreía. Su esposo la llenaba de regalos e insistía en que debían celebrarlo y le apretaba el brazo con fuerza mandando un mensaje para que sonriera. Ella lo recibía y sonreía. Invitaron a mucha gente y conversaron con la facilidad y el deleite de los que no dicen nada y bebieron hasta tarde. Cuando todos se fueron y la casa quedó a oscuras porque se debía dormir, Isolina caminó con cuidado por el pasillo y fue al cuarto donde hacía su planchado. También servía de despensa donde guardaba mercadería que encontraba barata en los mercados. Sacó los canastos de mimbre que estaban sobre la mesa, sacó la madera dejando sólo el armazón de la mesa con las cuatro patas. Dio vuelta la tabla y allí, fijado por cuatro clavitos, había un lienzo pintado al óleo. Lo miró un rato, recordó las muchas pinturas que había terminado desde que había entrado en esta casa—y que luego, sistemáticamente, había destruido—que contaban una historia que debía guardar tan celosamente como guardaba su tristeza de los demás. Volvió a colocar la tabla que formaba la mesa, salió con cuidado, cerró la puerta y fue a su dormitorio.

Cuando hubo pintado las margaritas, decidió agregar caléndulas y fresias. Sobre las baldosas del patio había macetones con geranios rojos y no estaba segura de si poner o no una enredadera a la entrada de lo que se suponía debía ser la cocina. Antes de cerrar la caja con sus pinturas dio un último toquecito a la glicina que apenas se veía detrás de un naranjo. Sólo asomaban tres racimos azules y ella tocó una de las flores con el pincel, sin pintura, sólo por tocarla. Había aprendido de las flores esa levedad del gesto, la caricia y la ternura en el movimiento, el modo de alzar la cabeza, recogerse el pelo, poner la tabla de la mesa con delicadeza otra vez sobre las cuatro patas. Había visto su vida en los pétalos de azahares, jazmines, rosas y claveles. Sabía cómo el sol acariciaba y las sombras cobijaban. Recorría el patio de los cuadros siempre anclada en sus glicinas, para no perderse, para no confundir su lugar que a diario se desdibujaba. Ella volvía al perfume, a seguirse en los caminos del jardín, entre el pasto y las higueras, el rododendro y las prímulas. Sabía desde hacía

Whenever she sold a painting, she would come home inexplicably sad. Like the day the art gallery awarded "Begonias" honourable mention, she barely smiled, while her husband showered her with gifts and was insisting they ought to celebrate, squeezing her arm, sending a message for her to smile, a message she would receive, and she did smile. They invited everyone to the house and all of them talked and chatted easily as people do who have nothing to say, and they drank until it was late.

When the guests left and the house was dark, because everyone was supposed to be asleep, Isolina carefully made her way down the hall to the ironing room, which was also the pantry where she kept the sale goods she found at the market. She took the reed baskets off the table and lifted the top, leaving just the four legs. She turned the board over, and there, held by four tacks, was an oil canvas. She looked at it for a long time, remembering the many paintings she had finished since coming to live in this house, paintings which later she had systematically destroyed, and which told a story she kept jealously guarded from others just as she had guarded her unhappiness. She put the board back into place, carefully closed the door, and went to her bedroom.

When she finished painting the daisies, she decided to add calendulas and freesias. Large pots of red geraniums sat on the tiled patio; she was uncertain about putting a climbing jasmine at the entrance of what was likely the kitchen. Before closing the paint box she gave one last little dab to the wisteria barely visible behind an orange tree. Just three bunches of blue peeked out and she touched one of the flowers with the brush, without any paint, just to touch it. She had learned that light touch from the flowers, the caress and tenderness in movements, the way of tilting her head, gathering up her hair, gently placing the board on the table again upon the four legs. She had seen her life in the petals of the orange blossoms and jasmine, the roses and carnations. She knew how the sunshine caressed and the shadows sheltered. She would walk around the patio in all her pictures always anchored to her wisteria, to keep from losing herself and her space which was fading away daily. She would turn to the perfume, and follow herself along the garden

mucho tiempo que debía salir, que este jardín no era el otro. Ella no entendía la violencia. Por eso se sentía mal hasta cuando una pintura no le salía como debía y tenía que retocarla, agregarle un color foráneo, una intrusión de amarillos en una violeta mal formada. No, no le gustaba hacerlo porque sabía que dolía, que la violeta nunca más se reconocería porque tendría heridas que no podría explicar y preferiría hundirse en el pasto del jardín y no asomarse con el único pétalo violeta. Hasta le parecía que algunas veces su pincel era como un zapato que pisara las flores. Claro que sabía que debía salir. Sólo que cómo explicar, cómo verse desde otra puerta sabiendo que todos hablarían, que el profesional admirado se salpicaría con barro como cuando se riega con fuerza en el jardín... por eso ella siempre destruía las pinturas de la historia, como él lo había hecho tantas veces hasta que ella aprendió. Cuando a veces se decía que quizás ella, por el sólo hecho de estar a mano lo había provocado... sabía que se mentía. Sabía que sólo había un paso entre su puerta y la otra. Pero, esta vez, como otras, volvió a sus comidas, a limpiar la casa, a preparar las camisas con un poquitín de almidón, y ya!

Quizás fuera porque la lluvia era finita y casi no hacía ruido sobre las hojas o quizás fuera porque se vio en el espejo y reconoció las señales del nunca acabar, o quizás porque sin querer llegara al cuarto que estaba a oscuras y supiera que podría ver las glicinas. Sacó del tercer estante de la alacena su caja de pinturas. Con seguridad encendió la luz sin importarle que fueran casi las tres de la mañana. Sacó los canastos que estaban sobre la mesa. Levantó la tabla y la dio vuelta. La colocó sobre el planchador, que era su atril, y lo miró como un encuentro. Su mirada era tan lenta que parecía que no sólo tocaba los colores sino que los ponía. Allí, una mujer rubia contra una pared de ladrillo. El cabello era espeso, en ondas, largo sobre la espalda, extremadamente artificial. Ella tomó el pincel y trabajó mucho tiempo cambiando no sólo el color del cabello, ahora castaño, sino también el largo y el estilo. Así. Ella. Así era ella. O mejor, así había sido ella. La mujer estaba obviamente corriendo y su expresión era de angustioso espanto. Los ojos agrandados por el terror, un brazo levantado para protegerse, el otro buscando algo para escapar, para escapar... Isolina le tocó la cara, besó la yema de su dedo y la

paths, between the grass and the fig trees, the rhododendron and the primrose.

She had known for a long time that she had to leave, that this garden wasn't the other one. She couldn't understand the violence. She was even unhappy when a painting didn't come out as it should and she had to retouch it, add a foreign colour, insert yellows into a poorly done violet. No, she didn't like to do that; she knew it was painful, that the violet would never recognize itself, because of its wounds which it couldn't explain, and that it would rather sink into the grass in the garden and not show itself with its single violet petal. She even thought that sometimes her paintbrush was like a shoe and trampled the flowers. Of course she knew she ought to leave. But how could she explain, how could she stand to be seen in another doorway knowing everyone would talk; the admired professional splattered with mud like when the hose is running full force to water the garden... that's why she always destroyed the paintings of her story, the way he had so many times, until she learned to do it. Even when telling herself sometimes that maybe, just because she was there, she had caused it... she knew she was lying. She knew there was only one step between her door and the other one. But, for now, as usual, she would go back to cooking, cleaning, dampening shirts with just a tiny bit of starch, and that was that!

Perhaps it was because the rain was a fine mist and touched the leaves making almost no sound or maybe because she saw herself in the mirror and recognized the never-ending signs, or because she simply arrived at the dark room unconsciously knowing she could see the wisteria there. She took her paint box from the third shelf of the cabinet. Confidently, she turned on the light without caring that it was almost three a.m. She took the baskets off the table, lifted the top board and turned it over. She placed it on top of the ironing board, her easel, and it was as if she saw it for the first time. Her eyes gazed at it so steadily they seemed not only to touch the colours but to place them there. There, a woman against a brick wall, her blond hair thick and wavy, below her shoulders, totally artificial. She took the brush and worked for a long time to change not only the colour of the hair, chestnut now, but also the length and the

aplicó a los labios de la otra que tenía ahora su cabello, el castaño original y algunas canas nuevas. Le tocó la mano de dedos crispados y delgados, sufrientes, de un marrón oscuro veteado con blanco grisáceo y le dijo "Hace mucho tiempo... ahora sí, es hora de salir." Con una destreza indescriptible, con una maestría de años, Isolina pintó una puerta en la pared de ladrillo para que la mujer encontrara algo para abrir y escapar. Y de pronto Isolina se encontró al otro lado, en el jardín, el sol de todas las primaveras pintadas tocándole la piel, sí, su piel, y se dejó acariciar por el descubrimiento de su fortaleza, de su resolución y saboreaba la certeza de una decisión final. Aspiró profundamente la vida nueva, otra vez, así, profundamente, y el olor de las glicinas le entró por la piel al centro del alma. Había esperado tanto tiempo para vestirse de primavera. Daba vueltas y vueltas y tocaba las anémonas, clavelinas, jacintos y albahacas, nardos y azucenas, hibiscos, gardenias y amapolas, pensamientos, lirios, dalias y gladiolos, todas sus flores la recibían desde distintas estaciones. Las flores azules que siempre habían estado al otro lado del cuarto oscuro se apoyaban ahora en la puerta recién abierta y reían en racimos, se sacudían y exhalaban perfumes, celebrando. Isolina llamó a Pepita "es hora de ir al refugio, al del jardín de las glicinas," y cerró la puerta al cuarto oscuro.

style. There. Her. That was her. Or, rather, that's the way she used to be. The woman was obviously running and her expression was one of terrified anguish. Her eyes wide with terror, one arm up to protect herself, the other groping for something to help her escape... Isolina touched her face, kissed her own finger and placed it on the lips of the other woman who now possessed her hair, in its original chestnut colour, only with a few grey hairs. She touched the clenched hand, its delicate, tormented fingers, a dark maroon colour with occasional greyish white streaks, and she spoke to her, "It has been a long time... now, yes, it's time to leave." With astonishing skill, mastery from years of experience, Isolina painted a door in the brick wall so the woman could find a way to escape. And suddenly Isolina discovered herself on the other side, in the garden, in the sun of all her painted springtimes, touching her skin, yes, her skin; and her newly found strength and resolve comforted her, as she savoured the certainty of a final decision. She breathed in her new life, deeply, again, like that, down deep, and the fragrance of the wisteria permeated her skin to reach the centre of her soul. She had waited so long to dress as springtime. Whirling and whirling around, she touched the anemones, the pinks, the hyacinths and orange blossoms, spikenard and lilies, hibiscus, gardenias, poppies, pansies, iris, dahlias, and gladiolas; all her flowers blooming from all seasons welcomed her. The blue flowers that had always been outside of the dark room were now resting on the newly opened door and clusters of them were shaking with laughter, exuding perfume, celebrating. Isolina phoned Pepita, "It's time to go to the shelter, to the wisteria garden," and she closed the door to the dark room.

Playthings

MICHAEL O. NOWLAN
Antigonish Review, 1988

Early January, the lone oak leaf
is a little toy
in the wind's hands. It is
brown against the crusted drift.
I watch
it leaping and crashing
against snow contours. In fun
fashion
it bounces up the shed wall.
Like a child, it proved
snow is for playing
in.

. . .

Oak trees thoughtfully leave
playthings
for January's wind.

This Body Is Growing a Person

SHEREE FITCH

In This House Are Many Women and Other Poems, 2004

Why say: I'm going to have a baby?
You give birth.
But you never own.
You never *have*.

To say baby is to say cherub cheeks and dimpled wrists
warm snuggle bunny baby bundle.
Sure there's a faint echo of crying and smell of baby shit
but both are sweet to ear and nose in conception.

Say instead:
This body is growing a person.
Picture that chalky fish on the ultrasound screen as
infant, toddler, child, adolescent
a grown person with a mortgage
no job, child support to pay.
Picture inside you a temper tantrum
a three-year-old scribbling on the walls
a face full of acne
a lip being stitched
a weeping teenager broken-hearted for the first time
a door-smashing wall-pounding adolescent
a runaway

an addict
a crackpot conservative, a lunatic lefty
a vegan
a vegetable
a prostitute
a convict
a schizophrenic
a tightrope walker, a high-rise window washer
a human trying to be.

Picture yourself inside yourself.
(Now there's a terrifying thought.)

For nine months see baby
an old person with false teeth, pleated face
halitosis, osteoporosis, a bruised heart.

Say:
This body is growing a person.
Be prepared
when baby stands before you
framed in the arch of a doorway
waving goodbye with a promise to call
a baby you can no longer hold
                    no longer rock
                    no longer kiss and make it better for.

Just watch:
as he goes out
into a world
that most days
is just not   good   enough
for any baby you might dare to call your own.

On Watch

(overheard at the bar)

ROGER MOORE

Land of Rocks and Saints: Poems from Ávila, 2009

The day I buried you, I threw my watch into your grave.
Earth covered the coffin: and my watch,
        a simple watch, face like a flower, ticking towards silence.

The clockwork of the universe melts slowly down.
Moon and stars will surely die.
The earth is just a heavenly body, heading for burial.

Silence: deep rooted in the earth.
Earth: where your body lies.
Lies: spider webs cover the clock hands,
        a tangled web woven by a silver tongue,
                        then silenced.

Dust to dust: a dusting of late snow
        brushed from the shoulders;
an hour glass turned upside down time's sand running out.
Your eyes being eaten by the earth, your bones unbinding.

Dust flies grainy, grates against the clockwork's teeth,
                the watch springs run dry.

[Je te cherche encore...]

PAUL CHANEL MALENFANT
Des ombres portées, 2000

Je te cherche encore avec des gestes lents de jardinier.

Ainsi va le poème sur ton visage.
En mémoire de toi.

Pareil encombrement de palmes, de pays.
Thym triste.

Ta marche comme une courbe de lagunes.
Hanches d'eaux tranquilles.

Je ne vais plus à ta rencontre.

Un seul souffle sur ton ombre déclive :
et tu disparais encore.

[I still look for you...]

Translation by MARYLEA MacDONALD
If This Were Death, 2009

I still look for you with the slow gestures of a gardener.

So goes the poem about your face.
In memory of you.

A similar jumble of palms, countries.
Sad thyme.

Your walk like a curve of lagoons.
Hips of still waters.

I do not go to meet you anymore.

One breath alone on your sloping shadow:
and you disappear again.

Rev. Elvis

JACQUELINE LeBLANC
Fredericton Daily Gleaner, August 11, 2007

Mike Bravener hopes his future has a little less conversation and a little more action. The former pastor in Fredericton has traded his clerical collar for a pair of blue suede shoes. He's an Elvis impersonator with a twist.

While his first desire is to entertain people, he also uses the allure of the king of rock 'n' roll to spread the gospel of the king of kings. "A lot of people ask me, 'So you're no longer in the ministry anymore?' But I kind of think this is my ministry. This is how I'm serving people. I'm out there singing and entertaining," Bravener says.

"I was singing at a ninety-year-old's birthday party. And my friend called me up, and said, 'Mike, there's a guy whose name is John and he is dying of lung cancer, would you come and visit him at his house? He's a huge Elvis fan. We're not going to pay you anything, but would you do it?' And I said yes. I felt it was a God thing to do," Bravener says. "So I went to his house and sang rock 'n' roll Elvis songs and a couple gospel Elvis songs and then he gave me this really cool watch. We did a prayer together." The man died a few weeks later and his family asked Bravener to sing at his funeral.

"To sing to people with terminal illnesses, and to do things for the Canadian Cancer Society, I just feel that it's God telling me to use my talent to make a difference in people's lives." He says he's amazed that by getting into a leather jumpsuit and putting on a little makeup, he can bring joy and a sense of normalcy in those people's lives for a few moments.

Bravener grew up in Ontario and always had a passion for performing. He and some friends used to put on Partridge Family shows in the neighbourhood. His family moved to Saint John when he was fourteen. He says he remembers seeing a man with a guitar in the park surrounded by girls. That inspired him to learn to play the guitar. "I always saw myself as a geeky guy, not popular. I thought, I'm going to learn to play the guitar and see if that's a good way to meet girls."

He taught himself to play the guitar by learning Elvis and Hank Williams, Sr., songs. He never worked up the courage to play in the park, though. His concerts remained within the walls of his bedroom, and the occasional campfire.

Bravener enrolled in theatre at Dalhousie University, but switched majors a year later. He decided he wanted to become a pastor, and a theatre major wasn't the way to go. His dreams of red carpets and performing were pushed aside as he fed his passion for God and religion. During his twenty-five years as a professional clergyman, he used his performing talents when leading youth services or while singing in worship bands. But soon, his passion for performing was getting stronger, and he started doing it outside the house of God.

Bravener had gone busking at the Boyce Farmers' Market with a member of a worship band he played with, and by the end of the day, he had lined up gigs to sing at parties. Soon after, Bravener started a sing-a-gram business where people could hire him to sing as a hillbilly, clown, or nerd for people's birthdays and special occasions. He eventually added Elvis to his repertoire after checking out the Collingwood Elvis competition in Ontario to pass an afternoon.

"It was absolutely funny," he says. "There were tall Elvises, skinny Elvises, fat Elvises. You name it. All colours and ages." He bought a goofy wig and added Elvis to his list of sing-a-grams. Eventually, though, Elvis took over and Bravener realized his talent to imitate the King was undeniable.

Bravener started playing gigs in bars and restaurants around Fredericton. He wanted to meet people who didn't necessarily go to church. "I started doing Elvis as a way to meet people, and my passion was to get people to hear this great message about God's love," he says. "And I thought if I was teaching the congregation to do that, then I needed to model it. Entertaining was the way that I felt God wanted me to meet people. That's what I did. I saw it as a part of my job to go out and sing in restaurants, or go to people's house parties to meet people who didn't go to church."

However, some people in the church felt that Bravener's side-business did not reflect well on the church. They didn't think it was appropriate. He was soon given an ultimatum, and he chose to leave his job as a pastor in July 2003.

"Some people say, 'You chose Elvis over the church,'" he says. "No, I didn't choose Elvis over the church. I chose the desire to follow what I believed was God's will, and that was to meet people who didn't go to church by using my gifts and talents in such a way that I can connect with them. So that's what I chose. I believe that I chose to be obedient to what God wants me to do, and that's to share my life with everybody."

In 2005, Bravener began supply preaching in a church in Southampton. And he still officiates weddings from time to time. Sometimes he doubles as the clergy and the entertainment.

But being an Elvis impersonator isn't always a godly experience. "I've been attacked by women," he says. "I was at an event, and it was getting later on in the evening, and they were trying to rip off my clothes. Their hands were going everywhere. I was being polite, because I was singing, so I was pushing them away."

Although Bravener admits the mobs of screaming women make him feel like he's doing a good job, he is a happily married man and would never cross the line. Bravener and his wife, Brenda, have four children: Andrew, Aaron, Maiya, and Josh, who is also an Elvis impersonator. He says his family has been extremely supportive of his choice to pursue performing as a full-time career.

Looking back, he says there were signs everywhere that his calling was to perform. He remembers when he was a young clergyman in Dartmouth, and he would use puppets and acting in his children's services. "These little old ladies would come to me and say, 'You missed your calling. You shouldn't be a pastor; you should be in comedy or in entertainment.' And I'd get so mad...But I think those little old ladies were onto something," he says. "Looking back, those little old ladies were the voice of God."

It might have been a long time coming, but Bravener is happy he followed his dreams. "I've met so many people who have given up on their dreams, and I keep telling them, follow your dreams. You don't want to be at the end of your life saying, 'I should have tried.' Try now. If it falls flat, and it doesn't happen, at least you tried. I can say, at least I'm trying."

The German Ball

PATRICIA PACEY THORNTON

A Room at the Heart of Things, 1998

The silk of my kimono clings to my wet calves. "I can't concentrate," I say.

"Still thinking about the Duke?"

"His name is Earl."

"Duke, Duke, Duke of Earl," sings Claudette. But she stops abruptly when she sees my reaction.

"Forget him," she says, biting into a bruised pear she has just taken from my bowl of fruit. "He's not worth it. Any man who can treat another human being the way he treated you deserves to have his pecker peeled, pruned, and pulverized."

"Appropriate punishment," I say as I rub baby oil over my neglected but now freshly shaven legs.

"That's just the beginning," she says.

"And I thought you hated violence as much as I do."

Push-pinned to my corkboard are the two colour snapshots taken by Claudette the night of the German Ball. In the first shot, I am standing alone in front of the polished doors of my clothes closet, dressed in an opalescent peau-de-soie gown and opera gloves. In the second, taken in the lobby of the women's residence, I have donned a borrowed fur-lined black velvet cape. Earl stands beside me, amused in his black tie and tails. My face explodes with pleasure—my cheeks bulge, my eyes disappear.

The movie-star Mercedes waited for us down in the Montreal night, black, and beyond it the red and yellow lights of impatient traffic.

"You look ravishing," Earl whispered in my ear, "'thou still unravished bride of quietness.'"

He hugged my gloved hand in the back seat as his father, a successful surgeon, weaved his way in and out through the cars as expertly as he might stitch up a lesion.

The Château Champlain, each crescent-shaped window ablaze with its own moonlight, shone like a lighted castle in the Black Forest. His hand clasping my waist, Earl guided me into the lobby and upstairs to the ballroom. A flurry of introductions followed—the German ambassador, his wife, the consul general—and as we posed for photographers at the dinner table, Earl encircled my shoulder in a possessive way. We dined, we drank, we exchanged silly stories, we drank some more. His parents frowned at us from the adjoining table when Earl and his brothers threw buns through the bouquets of balloons hanging from the ceiling. They'd never entirely approved of me, not since the day Earl told them that he was going to marry me rather than the German beauty they'd been hoping he'd marry. I was surprised that he defied his parents. Despite the fact that we'd gone out for a year and a half, we'd never had sex. His father, he told me, had warned him never to have intercourse before marriage.

"Your father was right to nickname you the Duchess," Earl whispered in my ear as he held me close during the first slow dance. "Will you be my duchess?"

Earl sat out the fast dances, but other partners—especially his younger brother, Helmut—sought me out when they saw the look of joy on my face as I swung and spun across the slippery floor.

"I love you," I blurted out boldly to Earl a couple of hours later in the high-ceilinged hall of the Château Champlain. We were taking a break away from the whirling figures in the crowded ballroom.

"No, you don't," he said, as if spitting out pits of an orange. "You don't love me. You just love the idea of a man."

"What are you talking about?"

"It struck me as you danced with my friends, even my brothers," he said. "Your face was beaming. You were having a wonderful time. *Any* man would do."

"But I'm happy because I am with you!"

Later we took a taxi back to the basement apartment that he shared with Helmut. Kitchenless, it had only one small bathroom, along with two narrow beds, each shoved against a wall. The focus of this dark apartment was the fireplace. We sometimes cooked steaks over it and always drank lots of Rhine wine. There was usually a case of wine stacked behind the bathtub. When we arrived, Earl started the fire and lit two candles. There was still a faint odour of late-morning fried eggs and German sausage.

I tried to tell Earl that I did indeed love him but my words seemed wasted. I would often use my body to demonstrate my love, and when we lay back on his bed, I would kiss and kiss him until my lips ached. Sometimes he would get carried away, undo my top and trace my nipples with his tongue. But he would always have enough control to say no at the last minute.

His withholding sometimes made me brazen. But that night we were dressed so formally that the bed seemed out of the question. And Helmut might come back with his date at any moment. They too would take a cab so there would be no warning of their arrival. We probably wouldn't even hear them when they came down the basement stairs. We would be face to face with them before we knew it. After Earl had poured us each a glass of wine and just as he was selecting some rhythm and blues, I came up behind him and embraced him. I moved my hands up and down his starched shirt front. As he began to respond, I turned him to face me. I took off his dinner jacket and threw it on top of the other clothes on the bed. I fell into his arms, and he began to tease me by blowing hot breath into my ears. My head bent back in laughter. He pulled me close—so close that I felt my breasts flatten against his chest. I kissed him, then unbuttoned his shirt. My fingers slipped through the stray hairs on his chest. I unfastened the cummerbund and dress pants and pushed the pants and underwear to the floor. I pressed my face to his pubic hair. I pursed my lips and began to peck his stomach lightly.

"I love you," I whispered.

He shoved my head down to his dark crotch. But at that same moment we heard the sound of people walking upstairs.

He staggered backward. "No!" he moaned. "No!" He pulled away from me and lifted his pants from the floor, fastened them, then said that we'd better go before his brother arrived. Then he poked the fire and extinguished the candles.

He barely spoke to me on the way home. We watched the traffic lights turn from red to green. Although we talked on the phone, even wrote letters, after the night of the German Ball we never saw each other again.

"Here, I'll have the apple if you'll have this lonely banana," Claudette says. "It's time to finish this still life. Come on, you haven't eaten a thing in weeks. You're just skin and bones."

Bones, bones. I can almost feel Earl stroking the bones of my face. "You will always be beautiful," he used to tell me. "You have such great bones."

I take the fruit but leave it untouched on the shelf above the bed.

"What you need is one of my famous massages." Claudette turns on the radio beside my bed. Like me, she's a resident assistant in charge of two floors of undergraduate students. She's also a physiotherapy student and is renowned for her back massages.

"My back does ache," I say as I hunch and then straighten my spine.

"Lie down," she says, licking the pear's stickiness from her fingers.

As I lie down, my face in the pillow, the towel unravels around my head.

"Pull your kimono down."

I ease the kimono off one shoulder, then the other, exposing my upper back.

"Further," she says.

"Do all your patients take their clothes off?" I ask as I push the robe past my lower back.

"Of course. Why do you think I went into physiotherapy?" She rubs her hands together to warm them and then places them on my bare back. "People are never so vulnerable as when they are naked. Hey, you're all tense. You're not used to being touched, are you?"

"No. Not for a while. What about you?" I ask.

"*Mon dieu*! I'm French. You know what they say about the French—we talk with our hands. We are much more comfortable with hands and touching."

Claudette, Buddha-wide, practically sits on top of me—her capacious hips straddle my thin ones. Then she expertly moves her hands across my back. My eyes close with the contact of her calming touch.

"How's Debbie?" I ask. Debbie, one of Claudette's students, leapt from her window two weeks ago when her boyfriend left her for someone else. All she succeeded in doing was ripping one ear off and getting her legs and arms lacerated by the cut glass of the broken window.

"Debbie's doing fine," says Claudette. And as she gently strokes and squeezes the muscles of my shoulders, she says, "You worry too much."

"When love leaves, death drives by," I murmur into the pillow.

"Your back's a mess," Claudette says. "It's all tight." She does a karate chop on my back.

"Can you feel those nodules between my fingers?" She places one hand on top of the other, exerting a lot of pressure as she goes up my back. "Those are tension knots. I've got to knead them out. I'll knead that bastard right out of you." She leans on me hard. Now I feel like a ball of dough being pulled and pushed under the heel of a baker's hand.

Her thumbs work in circular fashion on small nodules under the flesh on either side of my spine. As she presses closer, I am overcome by the smell, from above me, of ripe banana.

"You're not relaxing."

"I don't know if I'll ever be able to trust another man."

"'Trust the touch, not the tongue,' my English teacher used to say," Claudette says, and she gently pushes my head back on the pillow. I sink like a ball of bread dough that has just been punched down.

"Relax, relax," she tells me.

I try to concentrate on the massage. Having worked out most of the knots, Claudette now begins to vigorously rub my back with the palms of her hands. Her hands are as strong as a wrestler's, but as warm and fleshy as my mother's. I remember the times my mother would brush my hair when I was a little girl. It was baby soft but tangled too easily. She would stand as I sat on a chair and she would use her antique silver brush to get the knots out of my hair. As she brushed, my back would sometimes rest on her stomach; my head, on her breasts. I wanted it to never end.

"You're starting to relax," Claudette says. "Can you untie the front of the kimono sash? My hands feel restricted."

I open my eyes, lift my upper body and untie the silk sash of my robe. The front separates; my breasts swing free, and I lie back again. I remember the sensation last summer of my bare body bathed by the warm afternoon sun on a beach on the island, the soothing sounds of the sea in the distance.

"I need your love," Claudette croons with the voice on the radio and her hands begin to caress the vertebrae of my back. I can sense the satiny silk of my robe slide across my buttocks. She gently pulls it further down. Her hands start to massage my lower back, exploring the slopes and valleys of my body. My eyes close; my limbs loosen. I breathe deeply, drifting into a dreamy sort of doze.

"I'm going to use my fingertips now," she whispers.

I can feel her hot breath on my back as she leans closer.

"You know my mother told me her favourite thing for Dad to do was to kiss her breasts," Claudette tells me.

"Your mother said that to you?" I ask. "I guess I can understand that. I loved it too with Earl. But I wouldn't call it kissing. I'd call it sucking."

"You mean like a baby?"

"It's different. There's a little nerve that shoots right down to the other target area."

I remember Earl slowly caressing my breasts under my blouse, unfastening it button by button, unhooking my bra and then licking, sucking, and circling his wet tongue around my nipples.

Claudette's fingertips gently trace the curves of my back. The warmth of her touch carries down my spine and spreads across my shoulder blades. The fingers move along the outer edge of my back, down to my waist and then up toward my arms again.

I luxuriate. I relax. I realize how much I like to be touched tenderly, softly stroked.

Slowly the fingertips ease down my underarm, wend their way to my waist, then circle sensuously up my side. The palm opens, pauses, and brushes my breast. Fingers probe and press my nipple.

Suddenly I become aware of weight and bulk on my body. As Claudette crushes on my back, I feel like a clove of garlic in a press. I panic. I feel pinned and overpowered. I squirm beneath her. Claudette's massive girth grinds at my hip bones; the bones of my lower back begin to ache. I feel imprisoned, strapped to my bed, suffocated by my pillow.

"Are you afraid?" Claudette whispers, gasping for breath.

I shiver. I stiffen. I crouch like a cat startled by a sudden sound. I collapse like bread dough from an ice-cold draft.

My throat constricts. I am petrified.

Claudette shifts above me, heaves herself off my body and my bed, and stands up.

I sit up, pull my yellow kimono up over my back and aim my arms into the sleeves before I, too, stand.

Claudette looks surprised, hurt. "I didn't mean to— "

"It's okay. The back rub was over anyway, wasn't it?" I say, as I try to compose myself.

"Yeah," she says.

"I've got to get to work on this seminar." I run my hand through my hair and am surprised that it is already dry.

"Want me to pick you up on my way down to supper?"

"No. I think I'd better work."

"See you later," I say mechanically, as Claudette moves toward the door.

"Are you okay?" Claudette tries to look in my eyes. I look toward the full-length mirror. After she's left, I open my kimono and stare at my body in the mirror. My front is still white and cool but my back is mottled with red and warm from her touch.

Petersville

EDWARD GATES
Heart's Cupboard, 2006

I leave the keys to the van by the back door
and wait in the shadow of the old barn

prayers ripe with laughter lined
these boards with the earth's pull

slivered fingers calloused hands
queen anne's lace thick with the bee's hum

there's no rush I have a garden
a place to fall braille for the future

the grain grays and defies
the stain of warp and rot

the forest inside
rises to potential

In a Clearing by This River

VERNON MOOERS

Nashwaak Review, 1998

Among the moss and pine needles
        this blanket of leaves
I lay my head to rest:
We who came so far and loved
        for so many winters:
forever never lasts forever.
I put up no resistance now
am yours to do with what you wish.

You who walk through walls of fir
visit the resting places of your ancestors
walk softly on my grave
        quietly speaking
remember the wild roses of this place
how they blow in the wind on summer days
their smell in the morning rain:
transitory, my love
like the autumn wind;
when winter frost glazes
a small hole in your heart
place my hand over it
feel my touch rise up through earth
from those fiery depths
to burn softly in your hand.

Warmth in the Cold of a Strike

CARLA GUNN

Globe and Mail, February 13, 2008

I am an educator. But during the entire month of January, I spent several hours each day on the receiving end of a lesson.

Each morning, I would put on layers upon layers of clothes. When I was done, my body would be as rigid as a beetle's. God help me if I fell onto my back. I would then plop stiffly into my car—arms and legs sticking straight out—and drive to a place where other upright beetle people congregated. There I would drape a sign around my neck and join the procession. Hordes of beetles marching up and down, down and up the slippery, snowy, salty sidewalk, all locked out of St. Thomas University.

On that picket line, I learned about the depths of cold. My lips would turn blue to match my eyes, which in turn would run to resemble my nose. I looked like I was crying, which I was—on the inside. I learned how long it takes for your nose to freeze. The warm spots came with the hot coffee and delicious soups, and through those who waved and honked their support.

There were times, however—especially after the lockout became a strike—that people yelled at us and gave us the finger. Letters declaring us greedy liars and whiny crybabies poured into and out of radio shows, newspapers, and online meeting places. In a province where anti-union sentiment is too often palpable, solidarity is especially vital. And so we marched on. And on and on.

Now, *strike* is an interesting word. Here it means work stoppage. But it also refers to a blow or a planned attack. Certainly, this strike, which followed the first pre-emptive lockout of faculty at a Canadian university, was a blow. And what followed over the course of five weeks looked very much like a deliberate plan of attack, engineered to strike cold fear into us all.

It worked to a certain extent. We were indeed cold, but the kind that could be remedied by lying in a patch of sunlight or on a rug next to the heater with a cat on your chest. In reality, the strike mostly solidified us. Other unions, along with some of our students, braved the cold to join us on the picket line. A colleague playfully played the sax. Through laughing and sharing we felt much more the warmth of friendship than the cold of fear.

For me, the best part was that the shadowy figures I had passed in the hallways assumed shapes. I learned my colleagues' names and heard about their disciplines and interests. I saw elements of my own life reflected in their narratives, diverse stories but with similar themes, such as struggling to balance work and home. I discovered that in their "free" time, some of my colleagues were writers, poets, musicians, and filmmakers. I was privy to the endearing idiosyncrasies of a bologna aficionado, several martial artists, a Klingon, and a stock shark. They were academics, but they didn't live their lives trapped in the pages of their books. On the outside of those gates, I had never felt more inside.

But as the dispute dragged on, it took a toll. Money was tight. Our union was repeatedly condemned internally and in the media. The spinners spun their tangled webs and public support dipped. Some of our members allied with the employer. We started drawing lines in the sand. It got ugly—fist in the pit of your stomach, *Lord of the Flies* ugly.

Then a few days into February, the strike ended. A compromise, of sorts, was struck.

Now, back in the classroom, I have mixed feelings. I enjoy my students and am grateful for the friendships forged on the picket line, but I'm still angry about what I know now and wish I didn't. I feel uneasy around some of my colleagues. What to do when you meet at the photocopier? Look intently at your course outline like you've never laid eyes on anything so utterly fascinating?

This strike has left me stricken, wishing for healing—or an exorcism. But it would be wrong to banish my picket-line memories. I should keep them at the forefront of my mind. For it was there that I was privy to the many narratives that transformed one-dimensional people into layered individuals. Rumours may circle like soul-sucking Dementors, but nothing and no one is as simple as they may at first appear.

Just as I know that I cannot be defined by my position on a single issue, I know that each of my colleagues, regardless of his or her views about all that happened during that cold, cold month, is layered too. And although I may never agree with some views about this strike, in a liberal arts community, agreement is rarely the goal. It's about fostering free and critical thinking and respecting differences.

In moving forward we can add layers to create stiff, protective beetle shells or we can—through dialogue—peel and reveal as a means of moving us all to the inside, out of the cold.

Strike (v.): to strike up a conversation; to strike off in a new direction.

choo choo train

FREDERICK MUNDLE
Amethyst Review, 1997

the boxcars clickedy clack
into the fiery lake of the setting sun

looking like a long line of angry red ants
on their way to war   each door

seals souls in the mind   souls
on other trains tracking to treblinka

souls to witness firsthand the frenzy
of the demon-possessed in dachau

the moan of its horn in its wake
too   the packety-pack of echoing reports

of steel wheels on steel rails like shots kill
a boyhood longing to go where trains go

for i know i travel parallel to hell
when the ground trembles and the beast

of hades leaves tracks few will follow
and has cut ties too numerous to count

The Graduate

JENNIFER DUNVILLE

Fredericton Daily Gleaner, May 1, 2007

Not many people can invite great-grandchildren to their graduation, but "Mama" Alice Margaret Mokoena can. The seventy-nine-year-old will be the oldest graduate at St. Thomas University's convocation next week. It was her lifelong dream to get an education and it's an accomplishment she's happy to share with generations of her family and her university family. "I don't want my great-granddaughter to wait to come to school until my age," Mokoena said. "I want to be an inspiration to others."

Mokoena grew up in South Africa during apartheid when racial segregation was the law. Her family worked farmland, but it was unable to afford a formal education for all her siblings. Mokoena said she wanted to go to school, but her sister went instead because they didn't have much money. "At the time I thought it was too late for me and I was too old. I didn't want her to miss out because of me."

Life in South Africa was hard for Mokoena. She said she was mistreated by her husband and had no self-confidence. Two of her five children died at a young age and she had to grow crops to survive. But Mokoena never complained. She took in orphans and gave what little she had to them.

"One day I met a woman from Canada who saw that I was suffering," she said. "She told me about Canada and convinced me to go. I applied for my passport and eventually was able to come to Fredericton." Mokoena welcomed the change and didn't have trouble adjusting to life in New Brunswick. The local multicultural association and a church helped her settle in and prepare for life in Canada. "I kept asking when winter would come because I wanted to see the snow everyone kept telling me about," Mokoena said. "I put on the big coat and warm hat they gave me and I went outside. With my arms spread out in the air as the snow fell, I thanked God for bringing me here."

Mokoena spent her first few years in Fredericton volunteering at non-profit organizations, but her friends convinced her to obtain her high-school equivalent. She said the schooling left her with a hunger for more learning. "My tutor told me I was doing well and should apply to university, but I was scared. I didn't think I could do it because I am old and I had just learned English, but I thought 'What have I got to lose?'"

Mokoena became known as Mama Alice to students and professors because of her motherly nature. In her culture such a nickname is a sign of respect. "Other students seemed to enjoy having her in class," said Craig Proulx, professor and chairperson of STU's Anthropology Department. "She brought a unique perspective to class discussions and shared experiences from her home country."

Mokoena took a little longer than some to finish her degree because she had to make two unexpected trips back to Africa. One trip was for her sister's funeral and the other was when her eldest son passed away. "Mama Alice has had many struggles and difficulties in life, but you wouldn't know that about her," said Janice Ryan of STU campus ministry. "Her deep faith has guided her through. She has a passion for life and education and is an inspiration to many."

Mokoena will graduate with a double major in Human Rights and Anthropology and minors in Philosophy and Sociology. She is sad to leave the St. Thomas community because its students and professors are her family and its campus is her home. "If they had courses for great-grandmothers, I would keep going to school, but

I don't have the strength for such hard courses now," Mokoena said. "I will keep visiting, so my children [the students] will always be able to find me."

Mokoena plans to continue volunteering in Fredericton. She hopes to work for the rights of First Nations people.

The Cure

TROY FULLERTON
Connections, 2008

A poem
(lick this page

these cancerous words
are mephitic; each will
linger in the stink of your mouth [taste my tongue]
likely to eat through purities in your bloodstream
and slowly exalt you)
is nothing more, my love, than a
remedy for emotional anesthesia.

Rhodesian for Love

(For Rudo, a 150 lb. Ridgeback)

KATHY MAC

Lichen, 2006

Rudo rushes up larger than anyone ever
expected, doesn't come when called, doesn't
need to demand attention; after all, when that dog
lopes into a room, all sorts of disasters suddenly
arise, clear in mind's eye: unidentified flying
soups, fur garnishes for burners on max.

Really, it's no wonder sweet Rudo obsesses over
the strangest things—"Does this water dish
look safe to you?"—and ignores his keepers'
simplest desires; there's no collar yet made,
leather, choke, halter, spiked (outside or in),
that can stop one of Rudo's tender, ruinous assaults.

"Never again" you swore last time, and still
you let Rudo in, whenever he asks. We all do.

For Those Who Hunt the Wounded Down [excerpt]

DAVID ADAMS RICHARDS
1993

Bines had told his son this story. It was just before Willie went to bed. Bines was sitting, facing his son, with his huge hands folded near Willie's knees. Every now and then Bines would touch those knees with his hands, and draw them away delicately.

It was a story about a deer and how it outsmarted a hunter. It was a story of the woods, of gloom and darkness, of autumn ending and winter coming on.

"This happened a long time ago," Bines said. "There was an old deer, who had been in many battles in many ruts, and this was its ninth year. It had been cold all autumn, and the trees were naked and raw. Far off it could see smoke from the hunter's house, rising in the sky. It had lost its strength—this old buck—and kept only one doe, who had a small fawn. The afternoons were half-dark and winter was coming on hard—and the hunter kept coming—the hunters always keep coming."

Bines looked over at Ralphie and smiled, and Ralphie nodded.

"The big deer didn't have no friends. He usually travelled alone. But he saw all the other deer being killed, one by one. And though he gave them other bucks advice—gave them advice—they didn't follow it.

"So all the other deer was killed, one by one. But the hunter who tracked him—who tracked the old buck in the snow—was smart as any hunter. The buck knew this, and wanted to keep him away from the doe and her fawn if he could. He was on old deer and the doe was young. So the big buck decided to draw the hunter to himself—and each day the food was more and more scarce, and each day it was colder. And each day it led the hunter farther and farther from the cabin.

"The puddles were frozen and the trees were naked, and the sky moved all day long —"

Jerry touched the boy's knees lightly again and smiled.

"Every day the hunter would get closer—get closer to the doe. But the buck had a plan, which it had learned from living so long. It would always show itself to the hunter at daylight and lead him on a chase throughout the whole day. The hunter could never catch up to it. At the end of every day when the hunter came to the river the buck wouldn't be there. The buck always disappeared—and its tracks disappeared, as if it had flowed away."

"Where?" the boy asked.

"The hunter didn't know—didn't know. No one did. The hunter too was tired. He was a tired man. Each day he got up earlier. And remember—each day he wanted deer meat for his family. So he was only doing what he had to. Had to do there. Each day he concentrated on the buck—each day he followed the tracks to the river. Each day he found nothing there.

"And each day his children were hungry, his wife was sick. And each day the hunter was weaker and colder. And each day the big old buck had allowed the little doe and its fawn to live another hour, another night."

Jerry looked about the room, and the boy smiled timidly.

"The buck was old and tired but so was the hunter. The hunter had a bad hand and had wrapped it in his leg stockings. His eyes were fine and could pick out a small bird in a thick bush. He scanned the river every evening. The river was a wild river and had just made ice—a wild river there, but the ice was thin.

"One day after a heavy snowfall the hunter found himself deep in the woods—the sky had cleared, the stars was coming out—the hunter had been following the buck for many hours. It was hours I guess he had followed the buck that day.

"There wasn't a sound when the hunter come to the river.

"The day was solid and still and he cursed to think he had lost it again. Lost that buck there again. Now the stumps were covered and everything was quiet. Afternoon was almost ended—and night was coming on—and that's when he saw the doe. She was making her way along the riverbank, and he could just make out her brown hide by a tree. She was coming right toward him. It was almost dark. She hadn't seen him, and she was leading her fawn toward him up an old deer trail. The fawn behind her.

"So the hunter felt he must use this chance, and he knelt and aimed and waited. Everything was still. He cocked his old rifle and was about to fire—about to shoot it, you know. But then of course everyone knows what happened."

Bines paused and lit a cigarette. He smiled and touched the boy lightly on the knee once more.

"What happened?" Ralphie asked.

Bines drew on the cigarette and looked about.

"Everyone knows what happened," Bines said. "It has been passed down from generation to generation to all the smart deer in the woods."

"What happened?" Willie asked.

"The hunter aimed his rifle, and suddenly the ground moved—the ground under him—and the buck come up, from its hiding place under the snow, right under the hunter's feet—under his feet—everyone knows that—and snorting and roaring ran onto the river. The doe turned and jumped away, and led her fawn to safety.

"And the hunter made a mistake, mistake there—hunters always do sooner or later—I mean make a mistake there. He was so angry he didn't think straight.

"'I got you now,' he yelled, and he ran onto the river too.

"Now, that river could hold the buck, and it could hold the hunter. But it could not hold both together. And the buck turned and stood, waiting for him to come further out. The old buck never moved. And if he was scared he never showed it.

"And when the hunter got close the buck smiled—and the ice broke, and both of them went together—down together into the wild rapids—clinging to each other as they were swept away. And this story was passed down. It's a passed-down story.

"Now the end is going to come—in one fashion or another," Bines said, softly, and again he turned to Ralphie and smiled. "We all know, the end will come. You either face your hunters or run from them."

The Sea Breeze Lounge

AL PITTMAN

An Island in the Sky: Selected Poetry of Al Pittman, 2003

It's a warm overcast Bonne Bay afternoon.
There's a slight north-east breeze on the water.
Inside, Black Hat George is tending bar.
He, myself, and one other patron are the only
people here. The younger man has made his way
to the gambling machine with the aid of some
awkward machinery designed to keep him
upright. A truck ran over him in Toronto
and he's come home to learn to walk again.

The pool table stands staunch on its crutches.
The juke box is silent, all its hurtin' songs
sung to silence because pain can be fatal
and machines and people do break down.

Of course, I'm here too, about to give up
and perhaps give out for good. But for now
I'm one of three survivors who've almost
survived so far. Almost isn't a good feeling
but it shall have to do for now. You are
(my dearest darling, wherever you are)
surviving like the rest of us. I would like
to be of some assistance but the hazards

that have brought me here drag me down
like a heavy harness, an iron cross.

There's not much comfort but plenty
of solitude in The Sea Breeze this overcast
afternoon. There's a determined young man
learning to walk again. There's George
who wears his black hat with wild-west
authority. He has one leg left and a vigorous
hop in every step he takes down the seaside
street at high noon, sunset or any time of day.
And there's me, the picture of health
and wholeness (scared to death to stand up
lest I fall flat on my face).

I think it's worth it, whatever else our obstinate
ailments are, that we don't fall down, that all three
of us (and you) do our best to walk upright
and go with hope to wherever we are bound.

Right now I know we three could use a drink.
And this round's on me. But, most of all as far
from here as you happen to be this round's
a toast to you, your agility and your vigorous ascent
to the top of your dreams.

Acknowledgements

A book like this wouldn't be possible without the help of many, and we're happy to acknowledge their contributions here.

Our colleagues at STU assisted whenever we asked. Special thanks to Kathy Mac, who spent hours helping us think about and choose the poems included in this volume. (Of course, she had no say in the selection of her own.) Tony Tremblay suggested names of writers, served as ad hoc reviewer, and supplied information for the biographical notes. Stewart Donovan provided moral support and copies of the *Nashwaak Review*. Thanks also to Jo-Anne Elder, who provided important contact information, and Martín Kutnowski, our consultant in Spanish.

Staff members at St. Thomas also helped out. We're especially grateful to Anita Saunders for painstakingly creating electronic versions of all the selections that weren't already in that format. Mary Jones promptly provided biographical information on many of our contributors. Heather MacDonald Bossé, then Director of Alumni Affairs, gave the project a kick-start by suggesting names of writers, while Wanda Bearresto, Jackie LeBlanc, and Jeffrey Carleton all made valuable contributions along the way. Thanks, too, to the members of the Centenary Committee, chaired first by Frère Michael McGowan and then by Colleen Comeau, for their encouragement and support.

Beyond the campus, we'd like to acknowledge Joe Blades for helping with some of the poetry selections and Peter Ruddock for providing information for the biographical notes. A warm thank you to Susanne Alexander, Julie Scriver, Akou Connell, Paula Sarson, Angela Williams, Lisa Alward, Jaye Howarth, and all the other professionals at Goose Lane who helped bring this project home.

Nevertheless, our greatest debt is to the writers who sent in their work and then cheerfully endured the editorial process. Without them, there would be no *STU Reader.*

Contributors

HELEN BRANSWELL graduated with a BA in English Literature in 1978. She is the medical reporter for the Canadian Press. She received the President's Award for Journalism from the Canadian Press in 2002 and was a National Newspaper Awards finalist in 2004. She was named a Nieman Global Health Fellow at Harvard University for 2010.

IAN BRODIE was class valedictorian and graduated in 1996 with Honours in Religious Studies. After earning an MA in Religious Studies at Memorial University, he turned his attention to folklore. Since 2005, he has taught Folklore in the Department of Heritage and Culture at Cape Breton University. His doctoral dissertation is a folkloristic study of stand-up comedy.

HERMÉNÉGILDE CHIASSON is a poet, playwright, artist, filmmaker, and statesman. His book of poems *Conversations* (Éditions d'Acadie, 1998) won the Governor General's Literary Award in 1999. From 2003 to 2009 he was Lieutenant-Governor of New Brunswick.

FRED COGSWELL (d. 2004) was a poet, UNB professor, editor, translator, and mentor to many aspiring writers. A long-serving editor of *The Fiddlehead* and founder of Fiddlehead Poetry Books, he was the author of more than twenty books of verse. With Jo-Anne Elder, he translated *Climats* and *Conversations* by Herménégilde Chiasson, and edited and translated *Rêves inachevés/Unfinished Dreams* (Goose Lane, 1990), an anthology of contemporary Acadian poets.

SHELDON CURRIE taught in the English Department and played handball from 1960 to 1962 (in Chatham). Most of his career was at St. Francis Xavier University. He has written three novels, many short stories, critical essays, and two plays, including *Lauchie and Liza and Rory*. His story "The Glace Bay Miners' Museum" was made into the film *Margaret's Museum*. He was awarded an honourary doctorate by STU in 1999.

WAYNE CURTIS studied English through the STU extension program in Miramichi. He has published twelve books, including novels, collections of short stories, essays, and poetry. In 1993, he won the Writers' Federation of New Brunswick's first prize in fiction for "Fall of '58." He was awarded an honourary doctorate from the University in 2005.

STEWART DONOVAN has taught in the English Department since 1985. He founded the Irish Studies Program and the Film Studies Program. In 1994, he founded the *Nashwaak Review*, a literary, arts, and culture magazine that he continues to edit. He has published several books of poetry and a novel, *Maritime Union: A Political Tale* (Non-Entity, 1992). His *Forgotten World of R.J. MacSween: A Life* (Cape Breton University Press, 2007) was nominated for several non-fiction awards in 2008.

LORNA DREW graduated with Honours in English in 1982 and, after earning her PhD at UNB, taught part-time in the English Department for several years. Her publications include poetry, short stories, scholarly articles, and reviews. In 1987, she founded the Fredericton Raging Grannies. With her husband, Leo Ferrari, she wrote *Different Minds: Living with Alzheimer Disease* (Goose Lane, 2005). Currently she is a photocollage artist with a studio in the Charlotte Street Arts Centre in Fredericton.

JENNIFER DUNVILLE studied journalism and graduated in 2005. She is now the education reporter for the *Fredericton Daily Gleaner.* Her work has appeared also in the *Globe and Mail,* the *Montreal Gazette, Canadian Geographic,* and on CBC. In 2008, she won the Canadian Journalism Foundation's Greg Clark Award.

VICTORIA KRETZSCHMAR EASTMAN received her BEd in 1989. She has published non-fiction, poetry, artwork, and photos in various journals and chapbooks and co-wrote *Milo, Brownville and Lake View,* a publication in the *Images of America* series (Arcadia, 2009). One of her passions is collecting vintage clothing, some of which belonged to her Aunt Margaret.

JO-ANNE ELDER was a member of the Romance Languages Department in 1990-1991. Since then, she has taught French part-time and more recently has taught in the Gender Studies Program. Active as a writer, translator, and editor, she wrote *Postcards from Ex-Lovers* (Broken Jaw Press, 2005) and has translated many works from French into English. Two of her translations—a novel (*Tales from Dog Island: St. Pierre et Miquelon*, Killick, 2002) and a book of poems (*Beatitudes*, Goose Lane, 2007)—were shortlisted for Governor General's Awards. She is editor of *la revue ellipse magazine,* a journal devoted to Canadian literature in translation.

LEO C. FERRARI taught in the Philosophy Department from 1961 (in Chatham) to 1995. He wrote poetry, published extensively on human rights, and was an authority on Saint Augustine of Hippo. With UNB colleagues in Computer Science and Classics, he published a two-volume concordance to Augustine's "Confessions" (Olms-Weidmann, 1991). With his wife, Lorna Drew, he published *Different Minds: Living with Alzheimer Disease* (Goose Lane, 2005). He was co-founder and long-serving president of the Flat Earth Society; in 1995, he donated archival materials concerning the Society to the Harriet Irving Library.

SHEREE FITCH graduated with Honours in English in 1987. She earned an MA from Acadia University in 1994. She has been writing award-winning children's books for more than twenty years, beginning with *Toes in My Nose* (Doubleday, 1987) and *Sleeping Dragons All Around* (Doubleday, 1989). Her first adult novel, *Kiss the Joy as it Flies* (Vagrant, 2008), was shortlisted for the Stephen Leacock Award for Humour. **shereefitch.com**

DAVID FOLSTER taught in the Writing Program in 1981-1982; from 1997 to 2000, he was the first coordinator of the Journalism Program. His articles have appeared in many publications, including *Maclean's, Sports Illustrated*, the *Christian Science Monitor, Nature Canada*, and *Atlantic Insight*. He has published three books and currently is completing another on the history of cinema in New Brunswick. He was a founder and first president of the St. John River Society.

RAYMOND FRASER graduated in 1964 and has been a full-time writer ever since. He has written eight books of fiction, two biographies, five poetry collections, and a volume of memoirs, essays, and stories. His novel *The Bannonbridge Musicians* (Breakwater, 1978) was runner-up for the Governor General's Award. His most recent book is *In Another Life* (Lion's Head, 2009), a novel. **raymondfraser.blogspot.com**

TROY FULLERTON graduated in 2008 with Honours in English. His poetry has appeared in *QWERTY* and *Jones Av.* In 2008, he received the Robert Clayton Casto Prize in Poetry, sponsored by the Department of English. Currently he is an e-learning specialist with PulseLearning.

EDWARD GATES studied Philosophy and Education in the 1970s and later earned a BEd and MA from UNB. His poetry has been published in anthologies, chapbooks, and in three books: *The Guest Touches Only Those Who Prepare* (Owl's Head, 1991), *Seeing the World with One Eye* (Broken Jaw, 1998), and *Heart's Cupboard* (Broken Jaw, 2006). He lives in Belleisle Creek, New Brunswick, where, in addition to writing poetry, he instructs in karate and grows blueberries. **www.gatesbellearts.com**

MARK GIBERSON graduated in 1976 with Honours in History. Since then he has been active in organizational communications, including two terms as Director of University Relations and Alumni Affairs. Currently he is manager of Internal Communications for Health Canada's First Nations and Inuit Health Branch and principal of the Giberson Group, a communications consultancy based in Ottawa.

DAN GLEASON taught in the History Department from 1970 to 2000. He taught in the Writing Program and, as a photographer, documented many important university events, including Theatre St. Thomas productions and the construction of Sir James Dunn Hall. Now retired and living in Fredericton, he enjoys painting, gardening, cooking, volunteering, and kayaking.

CARLA GUNN has been a part-time member of the Psychology Department since 1997. She has published essays in provincial and national media; her first novel, *Amphibian* (Coach House), was published in 2009. As well as writing and teaching, she is a partner in Cogent Consortium, a psychology-based workplace consulting firm in Fredericton.
www.carlagunn.ca

RUSSELL A. HUNT joined the English Department in 1968. He co-authored *K.C. Irving: The Art of the Industrialist* (M&S, 1973) and has published journalism and scholarship in a wide range of journals and collections. He was a founder of the alternative journal the *Mysterious East* and of the Canadian Association for the Study of Language and Learning. On campus, he participated in the creation of the Writing Program, the Learning and Teaching Development Office, and the first-year interdisciplinary Aquinas Program.
www.stu.ca/~hunt

PATRICK JAMIESON studied English and Philosophy, graduating with a BA in 1972. He has published a book of poems, a novel, and two books dealing with Catholic history on Vancouver Island. He is the founding and current editor of *Island Catholic News* and is completing a series of novels.

GARY J. LANGGUTH received his BA with Honours in English in 1990 and his BEd in 1998. He has published poetry and short fiction in a number of journals and has served as president of the Writers' Federation of New Brunswick. He lives in Saint John, where he is a methods and resource teacher in the public school system and co-owner of the Fundy Gallery of Art.

JACQUELINE LeBLANC graduated in 2008 with a BA in Journalism and Media Studies. She was the founder and first editor of the *Forehead Review*, Université de Moncton's English-language literary journal. Her journalistic pieces have appeared in many publications in the Maritimes; some have been picked up by the Canadian Press. She is currently Communications Officer at STU.

PHILIP LEE has taught in the Journalism Program since 2001 and was director until 2009. He has written three books: *Home Pool: The Fight to Save the Atlantic Salmon* (1996), *Frank: The Life and Politics of Frank McKenna* (2001), and *Bittersweet: Confessions of a Twice-Married Man* (2008), all published by Goose Lane. He has been shortlisted for a National Magazine Award for column writing and has won numerous Atlantic Journalism Awards, including best magazine article of the year for "Sold!"

KATHY MAC (a.k.a. Kathleen McConnell) has taught in the English Department since 2002. Her book of poems *Nail Builders Plan for Strength and Growth* (Roseway, 2002) was a finalist for the Governor General's Award. Her latest poetry collection, *The Hundefräulein Papers* (Roseway, 2009), documents her adventures with canine friends. Currently she holds a SSHRC grant for a research/creation project titled "The Scholarly Long Poem: A Generic Hippogriff."

MARYLEA MacDONALD (d. 2008) taught French from 1995 to 2004 and was director of the ESL Program from 2004 to 2007. She was passionate about gardening, travel, conversation, and French. Her translation into English of Paul Chanel Malenfant's *Des ombres portées/If This Were Death* was published by Guernica in 2009.

PAUL CHANEL MALENFANT is the author of some twenty works of poetry, fiction, and non-fiction. His book of poems *Des ombres portées* (Noroît, 2000) won the Governor General's Award, and he has been shortlisted for Governor General's Awards on four other occasions. He teaches at l'Université du Québec à Rimouski.

ELIZABETH GAMBLE MILLER has published many translations of Spanish poetry and prose, including five books by Nela Rio. She is Professor Emerita at Southern Methodist University and lives in Dallas, Texas.

VERNON MOOERS received a Certificate in Social Work and a BEd in 1979. He has published a novel, *Briefly A Candle* (Fundy Productions, 1999), short stories, and several books of poetry. He has won many awards for his work, including Writers' Federation of New Brunswick prizes and the Grand Prize in Poetry in the Seoul (Korea) Metro Essay Competitions. He currently teaches English at Silla University in South Korea.

ROGER MOORE taught Spanish in the Romance Languages Department from 1972 to 2009. He has published short stories and eight books of poetry, the most recent of which is *Land of Rocks and Saints: Poems from Ávila* (Nashwaak, 2009). A 3M National Teaching Fellow, he has twice won the Alfred G. Bailey Prize for poetry.

FREDERICK MUNDLE majored in Psychology and graduated with a BA in 1978. In the same year, he won the Edwin Flaherty Prize in Creative Writing. He has published poetry in a wide assortment of journals, and, under the pseudonym babalabean, a series of children's books. He currently lives in Dalhousie, where he is senior pastor at Victory Lighthouse.

MICHAEL O. NOWLAN attended St. Thomas College High School (1951-1955) and St. Thomas University (1955-1959), graduating with a BA in Philosophy. Since then he has been a prolific writer of articles and reviews, and has published twenty books, including six volumes of poetry and several school texts. A major work was *The Knights of Columbus in New Brunswick: A Century of Service* (Faye, 2004). He was named a Fellow of the Royal Philatelic Society of Canada for his writing about stamps. A happily retired teacher, he lives in Oromocto.

AL PITTMAN (d. 2001) was a student from 1968 to 1970. In addition to six volumes of poetry, he wrote plays, short stories, children's literature, and songs. A native Newfoundlander, he taught at Memorial University from 1973. He was poet in residence at Grenfell College in Corner Brook at the time of his death.

NORMA JEAN PROFITT has been a member of the Social Work Department since 1999. She has written articles concerning women's issues, social justice, and education in both English and Spanish. Her book *Women Survivors, Psychological Trauma, and the Politics of Resistance* (Haworth) was published in 2000. She continues to visit and write about Costa Rica.

DAVID ADAMS RICHARDS studied English from 1970 to 1973, when he left university to become a full-time writer. Although known mainly as a novelist, he has written poetry, short stories, non-fiction, screenplays, and biography. He has won many important awards, including the Governor General's Award both for fiction (*Nights Below Station Street*, M&S, 1988) and for non-fiction (*Lines on the Water*, Doubleday, 1998). *Mercy Among the Children* (Doubleday) was co-winner of the Giller Prize in 2000. In 1993, he was awarded an honourary doctorate by STU.

NELA RIO taught Spanish in the Romance Languages Department from 1971 until her retirement in 2003. She has published many collections of poetry and prose, and her work has been included in anthologies, journals, and university courses in Spain and the Americas. Her work has been translated into English, French, and Portuguese. She is also a visual artist, having produced seven artist books and an award-winning DVD, *Francisca*. In May 2008, a symposium on her work was held in Gatineau, Quebec, with participants from five countries. She lives in Fredericton.

PETER T. SMITH graduated with Honours in English in 1993 and received his BEd in 1995. He is a provincial affairs columnist for the *Saint John Telegraph-Journal* and vice-principal of Kennebecasis Valley High School, where he also teaches English, psychology, and theatre arts.

CAROLE SPRAY earned her BSW in 1990 and has taught part-time in both the English and the Social Work departments. In addition to *Will o' the Wisp* (Brunswick Press, 1979), she has published poems, stories, and reviews in various magazines and is co-author (with William Spray) of *New Brunswick: Its History and its People* (Gage, 1984). Her children's story, *The Mare's Egg* (Camden House, 1981), was made into a film by the National Film Board. She is currently retired and living in Charters Settlement.

WILLIAM A. SPRAY taught in the History Department from 1968 until his retirement in 2000. From 1982 to 1989, he was Vice-President (Academic). He has published numerous articles, biographies, and books, including *The Blacks in New Brunswick* (Brunswick Press, 1972) and, with Carole Spray, *New Brunswick: Its History and Its People* (Gage, 1984). He is currently writing a history of St. Thomas University.

TONY STEELE was a part-time member of the English Department from 2000 to 2004. Much of his career was at the University of Manitoba. He has published poems in many literary magazines and in four books: *A Slanting/Line* (N. Young, 1966), *The Dance of the Minotaur* (Capricorn, 1970), *The Dancer* (Wild Columbine, 1995), and *Impossible Landscapes: Poems Narrative and Lyrical* (Broken Jaw, 2005). He is retired and living in Fredericton.

PATRICIA PACEY THORNTON was a member of the English Department from 1969 until her retirement in 2001. In addition to literature courses, she taught creative writing and administered the Department's creative writing prizes. She has published stories, critical articles, reviews, and newspaper articles. She lives in Fredericton.

ANDREW TITUS graduated in 1994 with a BA in Philosophy and English and later earned an MA in Creative Writing at UNB. He has been a part-time member of the English Department since 2005. His work has appeared in a number of literary journals and on CBC. His first novel, *Sweet Mother Prophesy: A Buddha for an Abominable Age*, was published by Broken Jaw Press in 2002. Currently he is working on his PhD at UNB.

TONY TREMBLAY joined the English Department in 1996. He has published widely in the fields of technology, film, media, pedagogy, and literary modernism. He edited *David Adams Richards: Essays on his Work* (Guernica, 2005) and *George Sanderson: Editor and Cultural Worker* (*Antigonish Review*, 2007). Currently he is Canada Research Chair in New Brunswick Studies. The son of three generations of mill workers, he grew up in Dalhousie.

DOUG UNDERHILL earned an Honours BA in English in 1968 and a BEd the following year. Before his retirement in 2000, he taught English, journalism, and writing at Harkins High School and Miramichi Valley High School. He has written eleven books, including poetry, books for children, Miramichi stories, humour, and sports. He was a freelance journalist for more than twenty years and continues to write an online fishing column. **www.dougunderhill.com**

JILL VALÉRY taught French from 1966 until her retirement in 2000. She has had a number of non-fiction pieces published in the *Globe and Mail*. She translated Nela Rio's *Sustaining the Gaze: When Images Tremble* from Spanish to French (Broken Jaw, 2004), and for the journal *ellipse*, she translated other work from English to French. She lives in Fredericton, where she is currently working on a book of short fiction.

DOUGLAS VIPOND joined the Psychology Department in 1977. He taught in the Writing Program and has published a number of articles and reviews on reading and writing, many of them with Russ Hunt. He co-edited special issues of *Poetics* and *Textual Studies in Canada* and has written two books: *Writing and Psychology* (Praeger, 1993) and *Success in Psychology: Writing and Research for Canadian Students* (Harcourt, 1996).

CHRIS WEAGLE graduated with a BA in English in 1998. He earned an MA in Creative Writing from UNB in 2002, and in the same year, received *The Fiddlehead's* Ralph Gustafson Prize. In 2006 he was short-listed for a CBC Literary Award. He recently returned to Fredericton after teaching for seven years in South Korea.

Credits

The editors and publisher are grateful for the kind permission to reprint the works in *The STU Reader.*

"Sold!" from *Saltscapes* (September-October 2007) copyright © 2007 by Philip Lee, reprinted by permission of the author. "Cop" from *In This House Are Many Women and Other Poems* copyright © 2004 by Sheree Fitch, reprinted by permission of Goose Lane Editions. "Lauchie and Liza and Rory" from *The Story So Far...* (Breton Books) copyright © 1997 by Sheldon Currie, reprinted by permission of Breton Books, Wreck Cove, NS, www.capebretonbooks.com. "Kim Hyo-Sung" from *Malahat Review* (Spring 2002) copyright © 2002 by Chris Weagle, reprinted by permission of the author. "Boxing the Compass" from *An Island in the Sky: Selected Poetry of Al Pittman* copyright © 2003 by Al Pittman, reprinted by permission of Breakwater Books. "Remembering SARS" (originally published as "Disease Crisis that Rocked the Globe Fresh in Memories of Those who Fought It") from The Canadian Press (March 6, 2008) copyright © 2008 by Helen Branswell, reprinted by permission of The Canadian Press. "New Waterford Boy" from *The Molly Poems and Highland Elegies* copyright © 2005 by Stewart Donovan, reprinted by permission of Breton Books, Wreck Cove, NS, www.capebretonbooks.com. "Parsley and Pink Petunias" from *Gaspereau Review*, no. 2 (1997) copyright © 1997 by Gary J. Langguth, reprinted by permission of the author. "Isabella,

Double-You Be" from *Event* (Spring 2008) copyright © 2008 by Kathy Mac, reprinted by permission of the author. "I Am a St. John River Person" from *New Brunswick Reader* (November 25, 1995) copyright © 1995 by David Folster, reprinted by permission of the author. "Et la saison avance" from *Climats* copyright © 1996 by Herménégilde Chiasson, reprinted by permission of the author. "And the Season Advances" from *Climates* copyright © 1999 by Jo-Anne Elder and Fred Cogswell, reprinted by permission of Goose Lane Editions. "Giving Up by the Goleta Slough" from *Impossible Landscapes* copyright © 2005 by Tony Steele, reprinted by permission of the author and Broken Jaw Press. "The Dialogue of Socrates with Hero" from *Nashwaak Review* (1995) copyright © 1995 by Ian Brodie, reprinted by permission of the author. "Fishbones" from *Ariel: A Review of International English Literature* 22, no. 2 (1991) copyright © 1991 by Roger Moore, reprinted by permission of the author. "The Mill Was All in Northern New Brunswick" from *Saint John Telegraph-Journal* (January 26, 2008) copyright © 2008 by Tony Tremblay, reprinted by permission of the author. "Yellow Bath" from *The Gray Door* copyright © 2004 by Patrick Jamieson, reprinted by permission of Ekstasis Editions. "Collecting the Stories" from *Will o' the Wisp: Folk Tales and Legends of New Brunswick* copyright © 1979 by Carole Spray, reprinted by permission of the author. "Elegy for Youth" from *Stubborn Strength: A New Brunswick Anthology* copyright © 1983 by Michael O. Nowlan, reprinted by permission of the author. "our love is different" from *STU Connections* copyright © 2008 by Troy Fullerton, reprinted by permission of the author. "Fall of '58" from *Preferred Lies* copyright © 1998 by Wayne Curtis, reprinted by permission of Nimbus Publishing. "Amanda's Presents, Returned" from *Grain* 34, no. 4 (2007) copyright © 2007 by Kathy Mac, reprinted by permission of the author. "Pride in the Name of Love" from *Saint John Telegraph-Journal* (August 14, 2007) copyright © 2007 by Peter T. Smith, reprinted by permission of the author. "Poolside North Conway, NH" from *River Poems* copyright © 2007 by Doug Underhill, reprinted by permission of Borealis Press Ltd. "Flying Home" from *Impossible Landscapes* copyright © 2005 by Tony Steele, reprinted by permission of the author and Broken Jaw Press. "Feminism and Education in a Flat Earth Perspective" from *McGill Journal of Education* 10, no. 1 (1975) copyright © 1975 by Leo Ferrari, reprinted by permission of the author. "On taking down an elm" from *Fiddlehead*, no. 227 (2006) copyright © 2006 by Andrew Titus, reprinted by permission of the author. "Reinventing Darkness" (originally published as "XXVII") from *Heart's Cupboard* copyright © 2006 by Edward Gates, reprinted by permission of the author and Broken Jaw Press. "The Man from Murphysboro" from *Nashwaak Review*, no. 2 (1995) copyright © 1995 by Dan Gleason, reprinted by permission of the author. "[Je pense aux livres]" from *Des ombres portées* copyright © 2000 by Paul Chanel Malenfant, reprinted by permission of Éditions du Noroît. "[I think about the books]" from *If This Were Death* copyright © 2009 by Marylea MacDonald, reprinted by permission of the author and Guernica Editions Inc. "Automatic Garage Door Opener" from *Schrodinger's Cat* copyright © 1996 by Gary J. Langguth, reprinted by permission of the author. "Of Particle and Wave" in "Roses, Poetry, and Prose" from *Journal of Progressive Human Services* 14, no. 2 (2003) copyright © 2003 by Norma Jean Profitt, reprinted by permission of the author and Taylor & Francis, http://www.informaworld.com. "November" from *Nashwaak Review*, no. 5 (1998) copyright © 1998 by Vernon Mooers, reprinted by permission of the author. "edmund somebody" from *Contemporary Verse 2* (1997) copyright © 1997 by Frederick Mundle, reprinted by permission of the author. "Up in the Air and Down" from *Fiddlehead*, no. 232 (2007) copyright © 2007 by Lorna Drew, reprinted by permission of the author. "The Inertial Observer" from *Grain* (2002) copyright © 2002 by Chris Weagle, reprinted by permission of the author. "Edna Remembers Exactly How It Goes" from *In This House Are Many Women and Other Poems* copyright © 2004 by Sheree Fitch, reprinted by permission of Goose Lane Editions. "Aunt Margaret" from *Echoes: The Northern Maine Journal of Rural Culture*, no. 52 (2001) copyright © 2001 by Victoria Kretzschmar Eastman, reprinted by permission of the author. "Little Napoleon" from *Grain* 34, no. 4 (2007) copyright © 2007 by Kathy Mac, reprinted by permission of the author. "The Call of the Father" from *Malahat Review* 112 (1995) copyright © 1995 by Gary J. Langguth, reprinted by permission of the author. "Slaying the Dragon" from *The Gray Door* copyright ©2004 by Patrick Jamieson, reprinted by permission of Ekstasis Editions. "J'aurais crié avec toi" from *Climats* copyright © 1996 by Herménégilde Chiasson, reprinted by permission of the author. "I Would Have Cried Out With You" from *Climates* copyright © 1999 by Jo-Anne Elder and Fred Cogswell, reprinted by permission of Goose Lane Editions. "From Combat to Cocktails on Clock Street" from *Globe and Mail* (May 13, 2004) copyright ©2004 by Jill Valéry, reprinted by permission of the author. "The Prince of Fortara and The Flat Earth" from *When the Earth was Flat* copyright ©2007 by Raymond Fraser, reprinted by permission of Black Moss Press. "The Gift of Life at the Wandlyn" from *Descant* 29, no. 4 (1998) copyright © 1998 by Stewart Donovan, reprinted by permission of the author. "Harry Forestell: A Man Ahead of Our Time" from *Carleton University Magazine* (Winter 2006) copyright ©2006 by Mark Giberson, reprinted by permission of the author. "Ode on a North American Desk" from *Fiddlehead*, no. 204 (2000) copyright ©2000 by Chris Weagle, reprinted by permission of the author. "St. Leonard's Revisited" from *An Island in the Sky: Selected Poetry of Al Pittman* copyright ©2003 by Al Pittman, reprinted by permission of Breakwater Books. "Historic Fredericton" from *Impressions of Historic Fredericton* copyright © 1998 by William A. Spray, reprinted by permission of the author. "Prairie Landscape" from *Impossible Landscapes* copyright ©2005 by Tony Steele, reprinted by permission of the author and Broken Jaw Press. "Playthings" from *Antigonish Review*, no. 73 (1988) copyright © 1988 by Michael O. Nowlan, reprinted by permission of the author. "El Jardin de las Glicinas" from *The Space of Light/El Espacio de la luz* copyright ©2005 by Nela Rio, reprinted by permission of the author and Broken Jaw Press. "The Wisteria Garden" from *The Space of Light/El Espacio de la luz* copyright ©2005 by Elizabeth Gamble Miller, reprinted by permission of the author and Broken Jaw Press. "This Body Is Growing a Person" from *In This House Are Many Women and Other Poems* copyright ©2004 by Sheree Fitch, reprinted by permission of Goose Lane Editions. "[Je te cherche encore]" from *Des ombres portées* copyright ©2000 by Paul Chanel Malenfant, reprinted by permission of Éditions du Noroît. "[I still look for you]" from *If This Were Death* copyright

©2009 by Marylea MacDonald, reprinted by permission of the author and Guernica Editions Inc. "On Watch (overheard at the bar)" from *Land of Rocks and Saints: Poems from Ávila* copyright ©2009 by Roger Moore, reprinted by permission of Nashwaak Editions. "Rev. Elvis" (originally published as "He's All Shook Up: Well-known Elvis Impersonator Mike Bravener Thinks of Entertaining, Bringing Joy to Others as Another Form of Ministry) by Jacqueline LeBlanc from *Fredericton Daily Gleaner* (August 11, 2007) copyright ©2007 by *Fredericton Daily Gleaner*, reprinted by permission of *Fredericton Daily Gleaner*. "The German Ball" from *A Room at the Heart of Things* copyright ©1998 by Patricia Pacey Thornton, reprinted by permission of the author. "Petersville" (originally published as "XVIII") from *Heart's Cupboard* copyright ©2006 by Edward Gates, reprinted by permission of the author and Broken Jaw Press. "In a Clearing By This River" from *Nashwaak Review*, no. 5 (1998) copyright ©1998 by Vernon Mooers, reprinted by permission of the author. "Warmth in the Cold of a Strike" from *Globe and Mail* (February 13, 2008) copyright ©2008 by Carla Gunn, reprinted by permission of the author. "choo choo train" from *Amethyst Review* (1997) copyright ©1997 by Frederick Mundle, reprinted by permission of the author. "The Graduate" (originally published as "Great-Grandmother's Journey Takes Her to STU Convocation") by Jennifer Dunville from *Fredericton Daily Gleaner* (May 2007) copyright ©2007 by *Fredericton Daily Gleaner*, reprinted by permission of *Fredericton Daily Gleaner*. "The Cure" from *STU Connections* (2008) copyright ©2008 by Troy Fullerton, reprinted by permission of the author. "Rhodesian for Love" from *Lichen* 8, no. 1 (2006) copyright ©2006 by Kathy Mac, reprinted by permission of the author. Excerpt from *For Those Who Hunt the Wounded Down* by David Adams Richards ©1993, published by McClelland & Stewart Ltd. Used by permission of the publisher. "The Sea Breeze Lounge" from *An Island in the Sky: Selected Poetry of Al Pittman* copyright ©2003 by Al Pittman, reprinted by permission of Breakwater Books.

Index to Contributors